I Know Why Old Men Plant Trees

Bob Seay

ISBN: 979-8-9867587-3-2

No part of this book may be copied, reproduced in any format, by any means, electronic or otherwise, without prior consent from the copyright owner and publisher of this work.

This is a work of fiction. Names, characters, places, and incidents are either the product of the author's imagination or are used fictitiously. Any resemblance to actual persons, living or dead, businesses, companies, events, or locales is entirely coincidental.

.

For Elijah and Isaiah

Contents

"A society grows great when old men plant trees in whose shade they shall never sit." — Greek Proverb

1

We stood at the base of El Capitan, the 3,000-foot sheer granite monolith in California's Yosemite National Park. Like most things in California, it was larger than life, unbelievably beautiful, and made for the movies.

We were well outside the splatter zone. I wanted to be far enough away not to hear the splat when some overachieving climber fell from three thousand feet. I put the wisdom of my degree in Risk Management to use and stood behind someone bigger than me.

We—the Algorithm Compliance Department of Peregrine Perch, Colorado—had flown out to California from Denver the night before. Leonard Bixely, our boss and the leader of our "not required but you'd better be there" expedition, insisted on this adventure.

"Don't worry, Wendell. We're not going all the way to the top," Leonard told me as I looked up. He sighed loudly enough for the rest of us to notice and gave the rock a wistful look. Rocks, of course, are unaffected by wistfulness; Leonard's show of primal longing was for our benefit.

"We're only climbing to Sickle Ledge and then turning around," he said. "It's about 500 feet vertical. We'll be back here before dark."

I was fairly certain a fall from 500 feet in daylight would render me no less dead than a drop from 3,000 feet in the dark.

"Think of Sickle Ledge as your own personal summit," Leonard explained while looking up. "That's what I did the first time I climbed here."

He casually moved a carabiner from the right side of his belt to the left while he looked at the wall. I wondered if there was a Subaru key hiding somewhere.

"Hey, Wendell." Leonard was smiling. Never a good sign.

"Want to make it interesting?" he said. "Say, a hundred dollars?"

"This is my first climb," I reminded him for what had to be the forty-seventh time. "How many times have you done this?"

"A few," he said. "But I'm not talking about you and me. Look around. Who do you think will make it to the top?"

He leaned toward me and whispered, "Or who's even going to make it to your personal summit at 500 feet?"

He pointed to the daughter of another one of the Compliance Officers.

"My money's on the kid over there," he said.

He didn't need to point. There was only one kid in the parking lot. She looked about fourteen and was all legs and elbows. She touched the back of her head with the sole of her right foot and twisted a full ninety degrees.

"Great," I said. "It's me against the lemur."

I considered my options. "What were you saying about turning around before you reach the ledge?"

"You can turn around anytime you want," Leonard scoffed. "Just jump."

Just jump encapsulated every feeling I had towards Leonard in that moment. It wasn't just the climb or even that particular day. It was the job. I was having a hard time being enthusiastic about landscape compliance. Just the day before, one of the Farrier Park cameras picked up a rogue purple flower brazenly blooming where it should not have been. The protocol was for me to investigate these things. I chose to ignore it.

My feelings had not changed on the flight out from Denver.

A group of guides approached us.

"Wendell Jones?" the guide said.

I raised my hand. "That's me."

My guide, Gary, worked with beginners. Leonard's guide wore a vest that said "Intermediate." Leonard seemed to be offended by the designation.

We lined up to begin our ascent.

As Supervisor, Leonard led by example and went first. Austin, an Animal Control Officer, made sure he was close behind Leonard, where he could immediately assume the lead if Leonard should fall. The animal control officers were generally more assertive than those of us in Landscape Compliance.

House Color Compliance could get nasty, though. They took pride in being the oldest and least flexible of the Compliance groups.

My job, as Landscape Algorithm Compliance Officer, was to protect Peregrine Perch from unauthorized vegetation—non-native plants and any flora not on the approved list or growing in a spot not authorized by the Algorithm.

Austin hunted marauding pit bulls and potentially rabid skunks. I battled ornamental grasses.

Other compliance officers paired up with their respective guides. They wore stylish, color-coordinated outfits and had obviously trained hard for this.

My personal training consisted of eating enough string cheese to make sure I was sufficiently constipated.

Gary and I brought up the rear, the physical manifestation of my inexperience with height, ropes, and gravity.

"Hold on," Gary told me when I was at the dizzying height of two feet off the ground. I would say I had a white-knuckle grip, but my knuckles only aspired to be wrapped around something like a handle. More like white fingertips that grew whiter when I looked down. When I looked up, tiny pieces of rock, disturbed by Leonard's shoes, landed in my eyes.

Gary pulled out his phone and took a picture of me clinging to El Capitan for dear life.

"Now hang on," Gary told me. He snapped the picture.

Gary had no way of knowing it, but I'd been hanging on since the first day Leonard was promoted to Algorithm Compliance Supervisor. My job was mind-numbing before that. It took Leonard to make it truly soul-sucking.

"I made sure to not get any ground in the picture," Gary said as I clung to the face of the rock. "Your friends will think you're a thousand feet up when they see it."

"Nice," I said. "But we could've gotten that same picture with my feet still on the ground."

"We could have," Gary agreed. "I just wanted to see how long you could hang on before you panicked."

"How'd I do?" I asked.

"You'll make it."

2

Gary carried the rope to our first belay, the bolts to which he would attach our line. He moved with the calm speed of someone who knew exactly what he was doing.

"On belay!" he shouted once the rope was secure.

"I'm coming," I called back. It wasn't what I had been told to say, but it seemed to work.

The granite felt cool against my cheek. I strained to see what might be above me, but there was nothing to see. Just a blue sky with a sharp black stone border.

There was no flag to capture.

To my left was Marisol, one of the color code enforcers, identifiable only by her bright red yoga pants. The pants were fashionable enough, but there are no flattering angles on a ninety-degree slope.

I tugged on the rope until I was confident it would stop me if I slipped. I was also fairly certain that if I did slip, I'd swing out like a wrecking ball and slam nose-first into the cold granite wall. At least I wouldn't ricochet and hit it twice in the same fall.

Squishy things don't bounce like that.

"There's no rush," Gary called. "Take your time. Make sure your feet are secure. Look for your next handhold. Move on when you're ready."

"You're paid by the hour, right?" I said.

"Actually, no," he said. "But you don't want to be climbing down in the dark."

"Put your foot where your hand was," Gary reminded me from above. "Use your legs as much as you can."

It took me about forty-five minutes to reach the first belay. It was a hundred feet off the ground and only about a foot wide, but it felt absolutely spacious after micro-gripping my way up the rock. Gary asked how I was doing, reminded me to drink some water, and checked my gear. Once I was secure, he started his climb to the next belay.

A vulture drew lazy circles across the sky below me. I realized I'd never seen a vulture from above, and certainly not while it was flying.

I wondered if he was waiting for lunch.

"On belay!" Gary yelled from above.

Naturally, I yelled back, "OK!"

"OK what?" he said.

We were clearly off script. Then I remembered my line.

"Climbing!" I yelled.

"Climb on!" Gary knew his lines. And, hopefully, his ropes.

The second stretch was a lot like the first. The rare moments when I dared to look down only made it harder to breathe. My forehead spent a lot of time pressed against granite. El Capitan had become my own private Wailing Wall.

Once again, I inched my way upwards while Gary waited patiently above. At least I hoped he was above. All I could see was rope and rock.

The second stop was a hanging belay. No ledge this time; just a vertical wall and some anchors. I clipped a carabiner to the anchor and hung in my harness. My calves appreciated the weightlessness; my thighs, which now bore my full weight, did not. I dangled there while Gary climbed ahead.

"On belay!" he eventually called.

"Climbing!" I was getting tired, but not so exhausted that I could not remember my line.

"Climb on!" Gary called back. He was sticking to the script.

As I reached for something to grip, I saw every pointless box I'd ever had to check off in the name of my career. I thought of things I wanted to do but couldn't. I remembered job assignments I had no desire to do but did. I remembered every landscaping violation I'd ever written and wondered how many pieces of my soul I had left.

And now I was risking life and groin because Leonard told me to.

I looked up and saw Gary waiting for me.

"We're almost there." Gary said. "Next stop is Sickle Ledge."

I glanced at my watch. At this pace, the climb would take another forty-five minutes to an hour—a little over five hours just for the climb up. Then we'd descend. The descent was supposed to be faster, which made sense. Gravity would be working in our favor. Until it didn't.

Since he went before me, I assumed Leonard was already on the ledge. I didn't know if he'd wait for us or if he'd just turn around and start his descent. At least he wouldn't be around me. Tomorrow's scheduled bonding experience was a group experience at a sweat lodge, which seemed redundant, given how soaked my shirt already was.

It took me just under five hours to reach Sickle Ledge. Leonard was already there, trying to persuade his guide to take him on up to the top. The guide was holding firm. I wondered if Leonard would sign whatever inevitable waivers were required to go on without a guide. Is there a climbing equivalent to leaving a hospital against medical advice?

As I stepped onto the ledge, I noticed a small plant. I pointed it out to Leonard.

"That pine tree shouldn't be here," Leonard said, as if El Capitan had violated some compliance code and I should write it up.

"And yet, here it is," I said. "And it's not a pine tree. It's a manzanita shrub."

You learn these things when you're the plant compliance guy.

The manzanita clung to a shallow patch of soil, its roots wrapped tight around a crack in the granite, much like my fingers had held on for dear life on the way up. The branches were twisted upward and sideways. Most of the bark had been stripped away. The bare wood that was left shined as if polished by years of wind, grit, and rain. Its leaves were small, thick, and dark green—stubborn, waxy ovals that hadn't shriveled in the sun or blown away in the wind. The whole shrub came to just above my ankles, but the gnarled trunk and crooked limbs made it look ancient; a miniature tree shaped by hardship and time.

It looked like something you'd see in a bonsai garden, but instead of copper wire and patient trimming, this shrub had been sculpted by wind, heat, and the indifference of a thousand tourists who assumed it belonged there.

It seemed disrespectful to call a survivor like that a mere shrub. On my authority as Landscape Compliance Officer, I promoted it to honorary tree status.

Leonard was right about one thing. The manzanita shouldn't have been there at all, which only made its presence more striking.

It was the most inspiring thing I'd seen all day.

"You think someone planted it here?" Leonard asked.

"I first noticed it last year. It's grown since then," Gary said. "I don't know how it got on the ledge. I can't imagine anyone carrying this while they climbed." Gary seemed just as fascinated by the displaced shrub as I was. I wanted to touch it, to somehow connect with this survivor and its independent strength.

"A bird probably ate a berry and dropped the seed here," I told Leonard. I looked up at him as I stood up.

"And you know what else shouldn't be here?" I asked. It was a rhetorical question.

"Me," I said.

"You can't just climb up here and quit," Leonard sneered. "You still have to get back down. They're not going to send a helicopter to pick you up."

I looked at Gary and hoped he would yell "on belay!" or "mountain lion!" or "incoming!" Anything so I could leave.

Gary was as silent as El Capitan and pretended not to hear the conversation.

"You're just tired," Leonard told me. He inched closer to me.

"What about tomorrow?" he asked. "The sweat lodge. Are you going to quit that, too?"

This was Leonard's idea of a motivational challenge.

I shook my head.

"No sweat," I said.

"So you'll be there?" he asked.

"No, I won't," I told him. "I mean literally. No sweat. No lodge. No sweat lodge. I'm done."

I adjusted my harness on the off chance that I might want children someday.

"You're already here," Leonard reminded me. "The hard part of the climb is over."

"Not the climb," I said. "The job."

The dumbfounded look on Leonard's face seemed to indicate that he needed more direct language.

"I quit," I said.

3

In my mind, I saw myself stepping over the edge, rappelling from my perch, and vanishing into the vertical descent.

The reality was much less cinematic. More like a sack of potatoes than Batman.

"On belay!" Gary called from below. "Ready to lower?"

I remembered my line. "Ready!"

"Lowering!"

I felt a tug as the rope lifted me off the ledge. Gary worked the line like a pulley and slowly brought me down. I was pure cargo at this point. Dead weight, with the fear of becoming deader. Pucker factor: 10.

I reached Gary in less than a minute. Then I waited while he prepared for my next ride.

"You don't have to face the wall," Gary told me. "I've got you. You should turn around and enjoy the view."

The pucker factor cranked up to 11 as I turned my back on the granite. I managed to suppress my fear long enough to take in the view as Gary lowered me to the next belay. I was on the ground in less than two hours. I thanked Gary for his patience, handed him a sweat-drenched fifty for a tip, and said goodbye.

Leonard's itinerary had us meeting in the picnic area for late lunch and a debriefing once everyone was down. The only debriefing I wanted was to change pants. I walked straight past the picnic area to my room at the Yosemite Valley Lodge, just on the other side of the parking lot.

I showered while I figured out how to get back home. I could wait and fly back with the others, but that meant a full day of avoiding Leonard and an awkward flight sitting next to him on the way back to Denver.

Or I could buy a ticket for the first available flight out of Fresno and leave right away. I went online and bought a ticket. I didn't care about the cost. At that point, I would have sat on the airplane wing if it meant getting away from Leonard.

The airport shuttle was closing its door as I ran to catch it. I made it to the gate in time to catch a very expensive flight to Denver.

The sun was just beginning to set as we flew over Grand Canyon. It was too dark to see anything after that. The lights of Denver welcomed me home.

I kept thinking about the manzanita on the ledge. It wasn't beautiful because of the adversity or the thin soil that it gripped for dear life. Those conditions shaped it, but that didn't start the process. It was beautiful because, in spite of being where it wasn't supposed to be, it held on.

It wasn't long before we were landing in Denver. I grabbed my duffel from the overhead bin and exited the plane in an orderly fashion.

I'd rushed to make the plane for the trip, so I stopped at a gas station off Peña to fill up and grab something to drink on the thirty-minute drive home.

Sitting on a counter in the gas station, in an unlabeled but truly "only in Colorado" space between buffalo jerky and windshield washer fluid, was a small assortment of bonsai: mostly junipers, a ficus, and one small, twisted manzanita with just enough bark peeled away to make it interesting. Like its cousin on the ledge, the tree didn't belong in that environment.

I took it home with me.

4

"So you quit your job?" Porter asked the next morning when I told him about my adventure.

Michael Porter was, in his words, "land rich, cash poor." He bought the house and ten acres of land in rural Elbert County—just half an hour southeast of Denver—before developers started moving in and prices went up. It wasn't in the mountains, but it was a thousand feet higher than the "Mile High City", with rolling hills and forests of Ponderosa pine. He'd held on as property values doubled, then tripled, and then kept rising. He'd had offers but refused to sell the land.

Money wasn't a real priority in Porter's world.

"Doesn't sound like much of a team-building retreat," he said. "If I were HR, I'd ask Yosemite National Park for a refund." He smeared tub butter on a cold pop-tart—his idea of a balanced breakfast—and washed it down with coffee and chocolate almond milk.

"We're out of creamer, but this really isn't bad." He took another sip as he picked up a clipboard labeled *Sunday*. Clipboards for the rest of the week hung on nails beside the fridge.

"Flint's vacation starts today," he announced to himself. He sat his coffee mug on Monday's reminders, leaving a coffee ring around Flint's name as if he'd circled it for emphasis. "Gotta feed their cat tonight. Snowball does not like to miss meals."

He looked at me.

"Speaking of vacations," he said, "did you bring me anything from El Capitan?"

"No, but I picked this up at a gas station on Peña." I presented the gas station bonsai. "It's a manzanita."

"Right." Crumbs fell down the front of Porter's "Pa's Dog Rescue" tee shirt. "Because nothing says 'personal growth' like a tree that can't get any bigger." He took a long slug of chocolate almond milk straight from the carton.

I counted three gulps.

"That's OK," I said. "I really didn't want any more of that."

I turned the tree around to look at the other side. "It was either this or an air freshener shaped like a banana."

"This is all just fascinating." Porter loaded what he needed for the day into a fanny pack. "But I have dogs to walk and a sourdough starter named Gladys across town to feed before Mrs. Duvall gets back next week." He took the last bite of the pop-tart.

"Business is good," he said. "In fact, seeing how you are now among the unemployed…"

"Voluntarily unemployed," I reminded him between chews, "but continue."

"Excuse me," he said between bites. "Seeing how you are voluntarily unemployed, want any dog walking gigs? I'm pretty busy these days." He looked at his clipboards. "I've got my usual dog walking schedule plus some extras tomorrow and I start horse sitting for Myers next week. That's always fun."

I was not ready to babysit a horse.

"I'm always getting calls from people on the Perch to walk their dogs," Porter told me. "I never take them. Too many soccer moms over there. Not enough cowgirls. I could just start referring those gigs to you."

"That would be great," I said. "Until I can find something else."

"No problem," he told me. "I'll give you some numbers and you can call them. Tell them you work with me."

Porter's dog-walking/pet-sitting business—which apparently also included sourdough starter care and other odd jobs related to living things—was all the income he had. That, and playing harmonica in a blues band on weekends, for which he was usually paid in jalapeño and mushroom pizza.

"I don't know why I'm so tired," I told him. "Must be the climb."

"Could be," Porter said. "I mean, in the past four months, you've lost a major relationship. You sold your home. And now you've lost your job."

"Voluntarily," I reminded him. "I quit."

"Whatever," Porter said. "But, yeah. Let's blame the rock."

"Hey," I argued. "Climbing that rock was serious exertion."

"I'm sure it was," Porter said. "But we both know that's not why you're tired." He tapped my chest with a guitar-calloused finger. "You're tired inside. Your inner light is flickering. I can see it from here." He held up his hands and drummed his fingertips across his thumbs like dancing lights.

"Flicker, flicker, flicker. Not good, Wendell." He scanned an imaginary audience.

"Somebody get this man a candle!" he yelled.

"I'm not flickering," I said. "Whatever that is."

"I once flickered, my friend." Porter flung his arms wide and then drew them back across his chest. "I was a flickering fool before I bought this place."

He put what was left of the almond milk back in the fridge. "I'll text you the number for a Shih-tzudoodle gig over in Peregrine Perch. Don't call her a mutt. They get offended over there. It's a 'boutique breed.'"

"I think they're called Shih Poos," I told him. "But thanks. I appreciate it."

"Tion, Liger, what's the difference?" Porter asked. "It's a mutt. And that's a good thing. The fact that someone needs a special name for it says more about them than it does about the dog."

He picked up a clipboard.

"I charge $30 an hour," he said as he looked at his schedule for the day. "Sometimes they tip, but don't count on it."

"Anything else I need to know?" I asked.

"There's a nice walking path in Farrier Park over there, if you decide you don't want to walk around the neighborhood," Porter said. "Be sure to bring some bags."

I knew the path he was talking about. I walked it every morning before work when I lived in Peregrine Perch. I wondered if the coneflower I'd seen on the monitor the week before was still there.

We'd walked that path. Angela and me. That ended when "we" became "me."

Porter texted me the name of the Shih-tzudoodle and her owner's number before he left. I recognized the name. Erica Martinez was a compliance officer. I wasn't sure which department, but I knew the name.

"I want to make sure you're a good match," she said on the phone. "Our old dog walker quit. Huh, Biscuit?" Erica's voice changed to that sing-song voice adults use when they have conversations with their dogs.

"So if this works out," she said, "it'll be an everyday thing."

I wanted to sound experienced, so I explained there was no charge for the first meeting or the first walk.

I knew where she lived as soon as she told me the address. Her house was in the middle of Peregrine Perch, in a row of McMansions facing Farrier Park. The park and the canopy of trees over the street made Farrier Parkway the showcase street of the neighborhood, even if most of the half-acre plots were consumed by a house, the driveway, and the standard three-car garage. Every front yard had an Algorithm-compliant flower bed that could include no more than two tasteful Algorithm-compliant lawn ornaments. Every lawn had either a pine, a maple, or a blue spruce. Additional trees were allowed by permit only and only if they met Algorithmic protocols. No other types of trees were permitted.

I went over to meet Biscuit that evening.

Erica opened the door before I rang the bell. Biscuit was standing by her side.

"Biscuit" is what happens when you mix a poodle with a Shih Tzu. She was the color of—well, a biscuit: golden in places, pale and floury in others, and a little doughy around the middle.

"You don't need to brush her or anything," Erica said, which was good because I had no intention of doing so. Her fur was as independent as she was—curly on her back, wavy on the sides, and straight as dental floss on her ears. It was clear Biscuit required more grooming than I did.

"I just need you to take her for her morning walk," Erica said.

Erica showed me where everything was—leash by the door, treats in the blue jar, water bowl beside the backdoor—and gave me the code to get into the house.

As first dates go, it was fine. Biscuit was shy at first, but warmed up to me in no time. You could tell someone had spent a lot of time working with this dog. I gave Biscuit some kibble and talked to her. She patiently waited for me to give her each piece, as if I were peeling grapes to feed to an emperor. There was no jumping, no nosing my hand for more. Only the involuntary wagging of a long, feather duster tail gently sweeping the hardwood floor. I patted her on the head and stood up.

"So," I said. "I'll see you and Biscuit tomorrow morning at eight."

"Great!" Erica said. "Send me a picture when you get to the chin-up bars on the trail." Erica was a "trust but verify" kind of person.

"Got it," I said. "One proof-of-life shot at the chin-up bars."

5

The next morning—the first day of my dog walking career—I walked into the kitchen just in time to see Porter dipping another cold pop-tart in the same chocolate almond milk he'd used as coffee creamer the day before. He looked me up and down, then drew a small circle in the air with his finger, as if he was marking a giant mistake in red ink.

"You're going to want to change clothes," Porter told me. He was wearing what he wore every day: naturally distressed jeans—the kind someone in Peregrine Perch would pay a hundred dollars for—a Denver Broncos tee, and a bright blue fanny pack.

I had on my usual business-casual button-down and khakis, with walking shoes.

"Yeah," I said. "I probably should. Now that I'm a professional dog walker and all."

"Dress for success," he said.

I pointed to Porter's most noticeable fashion accessory.

"What's with the fanny pack? Did the '80s drop that off on their way out?"

Porter rested his hand on the fanny pack like a gunslinger.

"Baggies," he said. "Dog treats. Snacks for me. Business cards in case I meet somebody. And it's easier to run in case I have to chase after a dog. I guess you could wear cargo pants, but who wants to jog with pockets full of kibble and a water bottle?"

He opened a drawer and pulled out a black fanny pack with the veterinarian symbol and "Elbert County Animal Clinic" embroidered on it.

"Here," he said. "Take one of mine. I've got a ton. That clinic is great for referrals."

I changed clothes and still made it to Biscuit's by eight o'clock. Erica was already gone, but Biscuit greeted me at the door, smiling and polishing the floor with her tail. She did a quick hop, like she was fighting off a case of zoomies, then remembered her manners and sat back down.

Biscuit's ears perked up when I put the leash on her collar. I gave her a couple of pieces of kibble from the fanny pack as a reward for her good manners, and we headed out the door.

I stopped on the sidewalk in front of Erica's house for a selfie of the two of us, dog and dog walker. Erica hadn't asked for a pic at the start but it seemed like a good idea. A dog-walker's version of clocking in.

Biscuit took the lead. She wasn't dragging me, but she did make it clear who set the pace. She marched across the park's parking lot like she had an appointment, alerting to squirrels but not giving in to the temptation to chase.

Like most of Peregrine Perch, Farrier Park was once part of a much larger horse ranch, sliced up and sold to people who wanted to "live in the country," but still have a decent Thai place nearby.

The giant sandstone sign read: "Farrier Park – Honoring those who shaped the land, one hoof at a time."

You could argue it was the horses who shaped the land. The farriers just provided the footwear.

I'd walked in the park a lot, but never with a dog. I assessed the course from a dog walker's perspective: a meandering mile-long ribbon of stamped, earth-toned concrete with the texture of a hairless cat for better traction on snowy days that ultimately led back to where it started. Lots of interesting places to stop along the way, for humans and for dogs. It was the epitome of Algorithmic perfection.

Ornamental kale lined both sides of the walkway, creating—according to the Algos—a natural barrier between people and snakes, while encouraging rabbits, deer, and other woodland creatures to dine nearby so suburbanites could feel like they were walking in actual nature.

"The Algos called this the "suburban-wildland interface." The snakes just thought it was a great place to hang out.

The kale and the pathway it protected wound their way past a pond, four picnic pavilions with benches, and several carefully curated wildflower beds. Three cement chess tables with benches were near the pond. Flowers were in plots or boxes along the path. Each species of flower had its own space, like animals in a zoo.

Prairie Phlox shall not lie with Black-Eyed Susan. Thus spake the Algorithm.

As Landscape Compliance Officer, I knew the park's flora, fauna, and any trouble between the two. My predecessor—the one who installed the kale that the snakes so dearly loved—once signed off on a patch of Mountain Laurel because he liked the name. He ended up with a herd of dead deer around the swings, traumatized locals, and a memorable feast for the neighborhood's stray dogs and cats.

About halfway around the track—on what locals called "the backside of the park"—I spotted the lone purple coneflower that I chose to ignore before the trip.

Echinacea purpurea grows all over Colorado. It's like horses in North America: Not native but so well suited that they might as well be. It even had its own official bed in the park featuring all the coneflower colors—purple, red, orange, and the yellow ones that everyone mistakes for daisies—each in their own cluster and its own nameplate. Because nothing says "nature" like an italicized Latin nameplate.

The flower's real offense wasn't being dangerous, but being out of place. In this park, that made it a weed.

It seemed like the perfect spot for Erica's proof-of-life shot. I made sure the chin-up bars could be seen behind Biscuit, took the picture, and sent it to Erica. I even managed to get the coneflower in the shot.

Then, without thinking, I plucked the flower.

Like it or not, I had become an extension of the Algorithm. I had killed the very thing I'd stopped to admire.

Biscuit looked disappointed.

"Don't judge me," I told the dog.

But I knew she was right to judge.

6

Biscuit only slowed down a little when we passed The Corral, the fenced-in dog park inside the people park. The place was clearly controlled by a gang of pugs who looked like they were waiting to take away some puppy's lunch money. Biscuit looked interested, but I doubted Erica wanted to pay me to watch her dog chase pugs for an hour.

It took us about thirty minutes to make the one mile lap around the park. Biscuit didn't look tired and Erica had paid for an hour, so Biscuit and I went around again. Then I headed back to where ranches were real and being a farrier was still an actual job.

Leonard called while I was driving home. I let it go to voicemail so I could ignore it later. I wondered what he'd offer me to come back.

I had several reasons to believe he would. Home gardening season was about to begin. I was the only landscape compliance officer in the office. Soon there'd be a riot of unauthorized daisies, sunflowers, and hollyhocks springing up around mailboxes and in other forbidden zones.

Without me, there'd be no one to verify violations or to send out the violation notices. The entire landscaping plan would collapse. Or at least I liked to think so.

Leonard didn't have much he could offer that might entice me to stay. Compliance officer salaries were set by an Algorithm with no room for individual negotiation. There were no real bonuses to be offered; just the Perch Bucks they gave us for Employee Appreciation Week, and those always expired before I used them.

The only meaningful change HR could really offer would be to get rid of Leonard. That did not seem likely.

I had enough money to get by for a while. Besides, I liked walking Biscuit. I understood why Porter did the dog walking gig. He could keep the horse stall mucking and feeding sourdough. I'd be happy to stick to the dogs in Peregrine Perch.

As I drove home, I couldn't stop thinking about the coneflower I'd destroyed. I was almost back to Porter's when I turned around and drove back to Peregrine Perch and on to Tuttle's Nursery on the south side of town. There were other nurseries around, but none of them carried as many kinds of plants and flowers as Tuttle's.

Ray Tuttle had the kind of tan you earn by not believing in dermatology, long sleeves, or hats. He was at the sales counter repotting a spider plant when I walked in.

I asked Tuttle if he sold coneflowers as singles. He led me to a tray of coneflower plugs, most of which were already in bloom.

Each one stood in its own cell like first-graders who'd been told to line up according to height. I picked out the healthiest and carried it to the counter.

"You're only getting one?" he asked. "Just one flower?"

"That was my plan," I said. I was making amends for botanical vandalism, not planting a garden.

Tuttle carried my one lonely flower to the front counter for me. I could tell he didn't think much of my botanical minimalism.

"It's just that people usually plant these in groups," he said.

I took the flower from his hand. "One is all I need."

"One coneflower it is." He rolled his eyes and rang it up.

It was getting close to what could be an excuse for lunchtime so I headed home.

"So how was your first day on the job?" Porter asked as I walked in. I could tell from the moment I opened the front door that he was cooking something.

"Thanks for setting that up," I told him. "Biscuit's a great dog." My eyes were watering from the fumes of whatever he was frying in his cast-iron skillet. I took off the fanny pack and set it on the kitchen table. I set my single purple coneflower beside it.

"I'm glad you like her," Porter said. "That's important in a relationship."

"I think Farrier Park's going to be our routine," I said.

"Ooh," he said. "Farrier Park. Very upscale. Did you remember to take a bag?"

"I did, but she didn't need it."

"Don't worry. She will." He laughed as he stirred his lunch. "The dog walking game isn't all glamor and adoration, you know."

Porter kept stirring while he looked at his spice rack. He picked something, sniffed it, and sprinkled it into the frying pan. Then he sniffed what was in the pan and sprinkled in a little more.

"Measuring spoons are for the weak," he said. He kept stirring and sniffing.

"Listen," he said, "it's going to get too hot to walk the dogs much after eight." He faced me as if to emphasize the importance of that message. "Not for you. For them."

He was right. The textured concrete walkway at Farrier was already hot when I put my palm on it. I couldn't ask Biscuit to walk on it with bare feet.

"I'll talk to Erica," I said.

"Make sure you do," Porter said. "Are the Regulars still there?"

I hadn't been to the park enough to know who was regular and who wasn't.

"Are you talking about the guy cutting the grass?"

Porter breathed in more fumes and added two more shakes of cumin.

"The old folks who hang out near the pond. Sometimes they're under one of the pavilions. They don't work there. They just...watch things. Got their own little social ecosystem. Kinda like pigeons, but with opinions and coffee."

"Yeah, I saw them."

"Good," he said. "They'll probably see you, too."

I wasn't sure what that meant.

"You might try the Corral they have there," Porter said through a fresh cloud of soy sauce steam. "The dog park part."

"We looked," I said, "but we decided to pass. She got enough exercise on the track."

"It's not about exercise," Porter explained. "It's about marketing. The People of The Perch like tiered price structures. Makes them feel like they've gotten something extra. You could offer 'supervised socialization at The Corral for an additional $10' and see what happens.

He turned on the vent above the stove and waved the fumes away from his face.

I opened a window. "Ten bucks extra for just standing around?" I said. "Seems steep."

Porter gasped and coughed from the fumes. "I would never get away with that here. But you could absolutely do that on The Perch. Over here, you'd be just standing around doing nothing. Over there, you're providing valuable security while Biscuit socializes with her peers."

He pinched some of the spicy eggplant, jalapeño, and garlic mix out of the cast iron frying pan with his fingers and popped it into his mouth. He closed his eyes and looked very satisfied for maybe half a second. Then his eyes flew open and dilated while his nostrils flared like a charging bull. He shook his head as he stomped his feet.

"Whoa!" he gasped. "That's hot!"

"What did you expect? I tried not to laugh at his pain. "What's in there? World War One mustard gas?"

"No," he gasped. "I mean fire hot. Stove hot." He grabbed his water bottle and took a long drink.

"Ouch." He did a full-body shudder. "But man, that's good!" He loaded his plate, piling the mixture on top of a bed of rice. "I'll probably regret this later." He turned and pointed the spatula at me.

"But a day without regret…." He coaxed me to finish the phrase.

"Is a good day?" I guessed.

"Is a waste." Porter took another bite. "Sure you don't want some?"

"No, thanks," I said. "I'll fix myself something less aromatic."

"Suit yourself." Porter alternated between chewing and gulping water, often both at the same time. "Yes, sir. You are Biscuit's emotional support human."

He pointed to the flower on the table.

"What's this?"

"Nothing," I said. "Just a flower I picked up at Tuttle's."

Porter wrinkled his eyes. "Don't people usually plant these in groups?"

"I'm going for a rugged individualist kind of feel," I told him. "The flower that dared to be different."

I needed stealth for my plan to succeed. I put on my black baseball cap and the most nondescript black tee shirt I owned. My weapon of choice was a small spade. I waited until it was dark and then took my solitary coneflower to the well-lit, algorithmically perfect confines of Farrier Park.

It was getting dark, but the park was still busier than I'd anticipated. Couples were walking, kids were on the playground, and people were walking dogs. A pack of runners circled the track. Some of the same retirees from that morning were still holding court by the pond.

The same old man was center stage for the evening show. I could hear them laughing from across the park.

My first instinct was to return to the scene of the crime. Unfortunately, a pack of parents with baby strollers were firmly encamped only a few feet away from where I'd plucked the original flower. I had to find another place to dig.

I ended up planting my coneflower alongside a bed of Colorado Columbine, in the shade of a sign that read, "Wildflowers of Farrier Park: Please enjoy with your eyes only." I made sure the coast was clear, dug a plug-sized hole, and tucked the coneflower in. I gave it some of my water and admired my work.

The replacement didn't look as defiant or brave as its predecessor. The freshly packed dirt made it clear that this flower was not a volunteer. And it wasn't as mature as the flower I'd pulled. But it was there, a proud, purple coneflower bathed in noncompliant glory, even if it didn't know it.

"I hope you enjoy your new home," I said.

"Butter is dairy, right?" was the first thing Porter said when I got home. He sliced off a pat of butter and stirred it into his coffee. "The creamer industry really is a racket," he said. He put the chocolate almond milk and vanilla soy milk back in the fridge.

"If I didn't know better," he said, "I'd think you had some deep secret."

I pretended I didn't know what he was talking about.

"I don't know what you're up to," he said, "but I'm going to the shed to play in the sawdust."

He stopped at the door and turned back.

"Some advice," he said. "If you're going to compost illegally, do it under a full moon."

7

The next morning, I walked Biscuit and scanned the ground for anything purple and out of place. I spotted a discarded wrapper from a candy bar and a purple hair scrunchy.

Somewhere in Farrier Park, a former ponytail was running free.

The flower I planted was gone. All that remained was dirt and disappointment.

I wondered if one of the Regulars had taken it on themselves to police the area. Or maybe some skateboarder saw it and did the same thing I did and just pulled it up.

Then I looked up and realized what happened. I'd planted my flower in front of the same camera that captured the one I'd seen the week before. The one I did not report.

"Amateur mistake," I said.

It was an unforced error, one that I would not repeat.

Biscuit stopped to take care of her business. I had the bag in hand, ready to take care of what I was being paid $30 an hour to do. When she finished doing her thing, I picked up her deposit with one of the doggy bags Porter had given me. I tied the bag closed, and we continued on the path.

We stopped at the next dog waste receptacle, as we were told to refer to them in Compliance. To civilians, they're poop cans. A small red light signaled that the motion sensor had notified the smart waste can of our presence. I tried to open the lid but it wouldn't budge.

The screen above the can flashed a message. "Unauthorized deposit attempted. Please scan the QR code on your bag."

I'd forgotten about this part. The baggies Porter gave me had no QR code. In my old job, I wrote memos about this stuff.

I was trying to pry the lid open enough to squeeze the bag through when I heard Leonard's voice coming through a speaker by the screen.

"Your unauthorized attempt has been recorded. Please deposit your waste outside Farrier Park."

We headed for Erica's and her mercifully low tech trash can. No camera. No QR code. No problem.

I dropped the bag in the can, let Biscuit inside the house, and made a note to get bags from Erica's before we left tomorrow morning.

"When did they start that?" Porter asked when I told him about my experience with the can in the park. "That's nuts. If you bag it, you should get to drop it."

"They started it when I wrote the memo," I told him.

"Karma," Porter said. "Whoa."

He handed me a piece of paper with a name and address.

"Want another client?" he asked. "Got a basset hound that needs walking."

"Does he come with QR-coded bags?"

I called the number Porter gave me and arranged for a free initial consultation with Churchill the basset hound. Churchill's owner, an older gentleman named Fred, insisted on meeting me at Farrier Park.

"Over by the red pavilion," he said.

"But I'll need to know where you live so I can pick him up," I explained.

"Let's see if he likes you first," Fred said. "We'll see you at Farrier."

I wondered if that might explain why the other guy quit.

I drove back to Farrier and entered the park. I could hear the voice of an older man begging someone to move from fifty feet away. The basset was just inside the Corral gate, looking up from the ground, his expression somewhere between obstruction and indifference.

"Fred?" I called.

"Right here," he said.

Fred held the absolutely unnecessary leash and spoke to Churchill out of the corner of his mouth, like a significant other might do when their partner is being particularly obstinate.

"There's a gentleman here to see you, sir," he told the basset in an exaggerated stage whisper.

Churchill yawned and then belched loudly.

"Ah, you must be the new dog walker," he said. He nodded slightly as he extended his hand. It was like we were meeting at a diplomatic event.

"Fred Allerton," he said. "A pleasure to meet you." He radiated affection as he looked down at the dog.

"And this is Mr. Churchill," Fred explained. It was a very formal introduction.

I bent down to meet Churchill at eye level.

"Ready to walk, Sir Winston?"

Churchill sniffed my shoes. He slowly rose to his feet and circled me for inspection.

Fred chuckled. "He can be a bit mulish until he gets used to you. Show him you're patient, and he'll follow when he's ready."

Mulish was generous. Mules moved faster than this dog.

"As long as he doesn't call a general strike," I said.

Churchill snorted and closed his eyes, signaling that negotiations, for the moment, were closed.

"Not to be rude, but…" I pointed to Winston. "Can he make it all the way around the park?"

"Oh, yes," Fred said. "He just does it at his own pace."

Something must have happened upwind, because Winston started tracking. Fred was obliged to follow because he was holding the leash.

"And what would that pace be?" I asked as I walked beside him.

"About an hour," Fred told me as Churchill gave up the chase and sat down.

"An hour," I thought. Half the speed of Biscuit. Half the number of steps.

"But he can't walk an entire hour." Fred laughed and patted Churchill on the head. "He really shouldn't go for more than thirty minutes. Maybe half a mile. Don't worry about making a complete lap." Fred rubbed the top of his dog's head. "Or you could spend the time in the Corral. He likes that."

"That's fine," I said. "We'll play it by ear and I'll just bring him home after thirty minutes of activity."

"It works for us," Fred said. "Can you guarantee that you will arrive on time?"

"As prompt as the British Navy, sir," I said. I resisted the temptation to salute.

Fred laughed.

"It's settled, then. Churchill and I will meet you. Want to walk home with us and see where we live?"

He lived only two blocks down the street from Biscuit's house. Even better.

I told Porter about my newest client over our lunch of falafel burgers covered in tahini sauce he'd made. It was either that, or some soy sauce, ketchup, and honey that was beginning to crystalize in their small packets that I found next to the spoons.

"How many dogs do you walk every day?" I asked.

"I've got five steady clients now," he said. "I walk two of them together and then I walk the three smaller ones together. One hour each walk." He walked over to his clipboards to look at his week. "Any extras, like people who are on vacation, stuff like that, I do in the evenings. Or early mornings. Whatever works."

"Why don't you have a dog of your own?" I asked.

"I don't know." Porter smeared tahini across a hamburger bun and then licked his fingers. "I guess I just never found the right girl to settle down with. Or boy. You never know."

He winked at me and then took a bite of falafel.

"You know how it is," he said. "Always a groomsman, never the groom."

Ouch.

"That's not entirely fair," I pointed out. "Sometimes I'm the best man."

Porter lowered his head, raised his eyes, and grinned.

"You mean like at Rigo's wedding? What was that bride's maid's name again? Oh, honey!" He took an especially aggressive bite of the falafel burger and grinned as he chewed.

But he was right. I was always a groomsman. Never the groom.

I kept thinking about my flower all afternoon while I helped Porter with someone's chickens he was looking after, and later when he checked on a feral cat holed up near the library with her litter of kittens.

"This one doesn't pay," he said. "But I like to make sure she's OK. Boots has been around here for a long time."

I thought about how happy I was when I planted it. How sad I felt when I discovered it had been taken.

By five o'clock, I'd decided what I needed to do. I rushed back to Tuttle's and arrived just as he was turning his sign from "OPEN" to

"CLOSED." He immediately recognized me as the guy who bought only one coneflower.

"Time for one more?" I asked.

"Did your flower decide it needed a friend?"

"Sort of," I said. Since I already knew where the coneflowers were, I went back and got another single plug.

Tuttle laughed softly when I took it to the counter.

"Another single?" he asked. "Really working on that Yard of the Year trophy, aren't you?"

"Something like that," I said.

Then I went to the park and planted it in the blind spot, beside the pole that held up the camera.

"There," I said to the flower once it was in the ground. "They'll never see you here."

I had made my small but natural mark on the world. Again. I felt proud, as if I was single-handedly making the world more beautiful. This must be how graffiti artists feel every day.

8

Biscuit and I were back on the trail the next morning, the dog for exercise and me to check on my flower. I felt responsible for it, like a hunter who shoots a deer and then realizes the doe was nursing a fawn. This was my fawn to feed; my orphan to protect.

The camera pole made an excellent landmark. My flower was just a few inches behind the base of it, where it got plenty of sun in the morning—when runners and dog walkers would be occupied and less likely to notice it—and enough shade in the afternoons to hide it from the more leisurely strolls of the evening.

After losing my first coneflower, I was glad to see this one still standing.

One of the Regulars, an older woman, kept looking my way. She'd look, then turn away, and then look back if she thought I wasn't watching. I told myself I was just paranoid. I was still adjusting to my new life of crime. I kept my head down and tried not to look suspicious.

By the time the track went past the Regulars, I was sure I was being watched. The older woman peeled off from the group and started walking toward me. Unlike everyone else on the track, she walked counterclockwise. A definite Algorithm safety violation. She was either brave, oblivious, or just didn't care.

We were only a few feet apart when a skateboarder cut between us. He clearly hadn't seen her and was not expecting a wrong-way walker. He swerved, scattering geese and nearly wiping her out. I dropped Biscuit's leash and grabbed the woman's arm before she fell.

Biscuit made sure we were both still standing, then ran after the reckless skateboarder, dragging her leash along with her.

I'd been a professional dog walker for less than a week and I was about to lose my first client.

"Biscuit!"

"Sorry, man!" the skateboarder called over his shoulder as he disappeared around the curve. I ignored him.

"Biscuit!" I tried not to sound angry. I didn't want to scare her away and have to chase after her. "Come on, Biscuit."

She turned around and ran back to us.

"You okay?" I asked the woman.

"I'm fine," she said. Her face was a bright red and her hands were shaking. I sat with her while she tried to catch her breath. Biscuit put her head in the woman's lap. She rubbed Biscuit's ear while I contemplated the healing power of dogs.

"Go on, finish your walk," she said. "I'm fine, really. Thank you." She gave Biscuit a gentle pat.

"Good girl."

One of the Regulars, an older gentleman, was walking toward us.

"Looks like your friend is on his way." I stood. "Are you going to be OK if I leave?"

"Yes." She leaned closer to me.

"I saw your pretty purple flower," she whispered.

"What?" I said. "I don't have any flowers."

She patted my hand.

"None of us do, honey."

"You okay?" the man asked as soon as he reached our bench.

"I'm fine," the woman said. She thanked me and I watched them walk back to the pavilion with the other Regulars.

By the time I dropped off Biscuit and had begged, bribed, and dragged Churchill a quarter of the way around the track, the woman who almost got run over by the skateboarder had moved back to the bench where I left her. She waved at me as we walked by.

Churchill wasn't in a hurry, so I checked on her.

"You all right? That was scary back there."

"Act like you don't know me," she whispered.

"But I don't know you," I said.

"Even better." The old woman motioned me closer. It took a trail of Fred's homemade beef jerky to get Churchill within range, but at least I didn't have to worry about him running off.

"The city fined my neighbor $500 for planting a rosebush in his backyard," she told me. "Said it was some kind of Algo-something landscape violation."

"Algorithmic," I said. I bit my lower lip and nodded my head. "Probably an Algorithmic Landscape Violation."

"Whatever," she said. She motioned me closer, like she wanted to share a secret.

I dropped Churchill's leash and joined her on the bench. It wasn't like I was going to have to chase him. And he had jerky to chew.

"They posted his name in the newsletter," she told me "You would have thought the poor man was a criminal the way people treated him after that. He ended up moving to Colorado Springs to live with his son."

I felt the reflexes from my former job kick in.

"Was he over the quota for rosebushes per city block?" I asked.

She looked shocked that I would even say such a thing. Honestly, so was I.

"Sorry," I said. "I'm sorry to hear about your friend."

I remembered the case because I was the one who verified the violation and sent out the notice. It was Mr. Johnson's third offense. He got the maximum penalty and special recognition in that week's violations report in the newsletter.

Roses aren't invasive. They certainly aren't weeds. But the Algorithm had a quota for roses, and this cul-de-sac had met it. Mr. Johnson's rose made one too many.

In Peregrine Perch, that made it a weed.

I wrote the article that ran in the newsletter alongside the weekly violation report, a hit piece called "Know Your Invasive Species—and the Neighbors Who Bring Them In."

I didn't actually *write* it. I entered the data and AI wrote it. The Algorithm required all communications, notifications, schoolwork, anything that another person might read for any reason, to be written by artificial intelligence. Unfiltered human communication was considered noncompliant and a violation of the Algorithm Language Compliance protocols, subject to whatever financial penalty Leonard felt like inflicting.

Leonard placed my article next to the week's list of violators, making every infraction sound more criminal than it was. Someone could've been fined for planting daisies. Or it could've been dodder—a parasitic orange or yellow vine that strangles everything it touches and survives by draining the life from its host.

Much like Leonard.

It didn't matter what the plant was. A violation was a violation.

I'd told myself I was just doing my job. But now, after hearing about what my job had done to Mr. Johnson's life, I wasn't so sure it was the right thing to do. I wondered if this is how attack drone pilots felt when the camera catches their target's face right before the missile hits.

"Then again," I told the woman, "the quota for rogue coneflowers in Farrier Park is zero, but it's still here."

Her pale face grew even paler. She studied me for a second, and then almost smiled.

"Exactly," she said, as if talking to a morally stunted child. "But some rules can be bent, especially when they make no sense. Like this Algo-whatever business."

I realized I might have just confessed to a crime. I hoped she wasn't a mandated reporter, but at her age, that seemed unlikely.

"But I don't know what you're talking about." I made sure to smile as I lied. I stood up to go.

"I asked Monica about it," Ida said. "She told me I could always talk to City Council."

I smiled. "You should do that," I told her.

I didn't know who Monica was, but Leonard's disdain for City Council and the Mayor's office in general was an open secret among the Compliance Officers and a loudly whispered rumor among most of the community. It had been that way for as long as I had worked in Compliance; it didn't matter who was mayor or who was on City Council. City Council's position was that they and the Mayor were elected to run the city. Leonard argued that he and the Algos were there before the city officials were elected and they would be there after this group of city officials was gone.

"Why are you telling me this?" I asked.

"No reason," Ida said. "Just passing the time." She leaned on me as I helped her to her feet. "Thank you for helping me before. You're a good man." She looked me up and down.

"Are you single?" she asked. "You might like my daughter."

I smiled. "If you're OK, then I need to get Churchill moving again."

Churchill and I finished his thirty minutes of activity, which probably included about twenty minutes of actual walking and another ten of Churchill considering what he wished to do next. By the time we made it back to his house, our half-hour had been over for several minutes.

I thought about Mr. Johnson as I drove home. If Leonard fined him $500 for a rosebush in his own backyard, how much more would he fine me when he needed to make another example?

I relayed all of this to Porter while he was bathing a Saint Bernard named Bernie.

"You need to be careful," Porter said. Bernie did a full body shake, drenching Porter, me, and everything in the bathroom.

"Between this and the baggie incident, you're going to get yourself banned from the park."

"And there goes my ginormous sixty dollars a day," I said.

Porter stopped scrubbing and looked at me.

"And there go my referrals." He went back to scrubbing the Saint Bernard.

"Oh, man," I said. "Didn't even think of that."

"Twelve hundred bucks a month is not pocket change," Porter reminded me. "At least, not for my pockets."

"Sorry."

He grinned. "Don't worry too much about it," he said. "I quit walking at Farrier Park years ago. Not my crowd. That's why I gave those gigs to you."

"Still, people talk," I said. "You don't need that."

"Exactly."

Porter helped Bernie out of the tub, meaning he stopped holding the beast down and got out of the way while the Saint Bernard leaped over the sides of the clawfoot bathtub and shook water all over the bathroom.

Porter led Bernie to his crate and started mopping the floor. I grabbed a towel to help—there was enough water for both of us.

9

"On a totally unrelated note," Porter said as he mopped up after the Saint Bernard, "Pa from Pa's Dog Rescue called me this morning. He's desperate to find a foster for an Australian Shepherd. I told him we might be interested."

I gave him a look. "We?"

Porter shrugged and tossed the towel in the laundry.

"You live here, don't you? This will affect you, too. We're talking commitment, Wendell. Commitment. This isn't one of your bridesmaids. You don't take on something like this and just abandon it the next day. That's how dogs end up at Pa's in the first place."

"Aren't Aussies really smart?" I'd been around enough smart dogs to know what that meant. "And really destructive?"

"They can be." Porter gathered up towels, tossing one at the rim of the tub. "Ever seen an Aussie work cattle?"

He started laughing. "I was subbing up at the elementary school a few years ago. Second grade. I had to walk the kids over to the gym for PE. This Aussie shows up and starts herding the kids who were messing around at the back of the line."

"How did the kids react?"

"They screamed." He laughed. "And ran, which was the wrong thing to do. Then the gym teacher shows up, so now he's chasing the dog. Then the principal comes walking across the playground, coming back from a meeting or something."

Porter is laughing so hard he's having a hard time telling the story.

"The principal doesn't have a clue," he continued. "He sees all of this and starts yelling and chasing the dog. Meanwhile, the school secretary's out there, screaming and waving her arms like she's flagging down a bus."

I ducked to avoid being hit by Porter's flailing hands.

"What are you doing all this time?" I managed to get out.

"I'm looking around for the owner," he said. "And wondering how this dog got loose and if this guy's going to show up."

Porter wiped his face with a towel.

"I'm going to have to change shirts," he said. "I should have done this naked."

"Did not need that image," I told him and tried not to shudder. "So, back to the dog."

"Oh, yeah. Well, the dog's got all these kids herded into a tight little circle and he's moving them toward the gym like he knows what he's doing. I'm dying. The owner finally shows up, just strolls over like this is an everyday thing, no big deal, and says, 'That'll do.'"

Porter wiped tears from his eyes.

"The dog stops what he's doing and just walks over to this guy, like he's clocking out and going home from work. The owner says 'load up!' and the dog jumps right into the back of his truck. Lays down like nothing happened."

"Anybody hurt?" I asked.

"Naw," he said. "Nobody hurt."

"What happened to the dog?"

Porter shook his head.

"The principal said he was being aggressive and tried to have him put down," he explained. "But he wasn't being aggressive. He was being an Aussie."

Porter looked at the floor as he mopped up more water that was once on the Saint Bernard.

"Did they put the dog down?" I asked.

"No." Porter looked up at me as he wiped the floor. "The owner apologized. The two of us, we convinced the principal to let him go."

He wrung out a towel over the tub.

"Aussies like that are amazing," he said. "Worth at least two men on a ranch. And they won't complain about the pay or try to sleep with your wife. But they will destroy a house if you let them."

I pictured my shoes, couch, and whatever dignity I had left after this last year, chewed to bits.

"How much damage are we talking?"

He grinned. "Depends. If he's bored, you'll know. But they're not bad dogs. Seriously. There are no bad dogs. Just bad owners. Or bad situations. Just like you with that compliance gig. No difference."

I ignored the reference to my own work-related acting out.

"Great," I said. "So, the plan is to keep him busy and hope he doesn't eat the furniture."

Porter nodded. "Exactly."

"And does this dog that we're bringing into our home have a name?"

"Banjo. Like the instrument." Porter pretended to play, spun around, and gave me a theatrical bow before leaning on the counter and wiping his face again.

"These people don't know what they've got," he said. "This dog is six months old—still young enough to start training. They bought him as a puppy, for a pet, because that's how they think of dogs. But if they worked with him, or got a trainer, they could sell him to a rancher for a couple grand, easy. Trainers pay a lot for pups with the right instincts."

He tossed a third towel into the laundry basket while he spoke. "You can't turn a dog like that into a houseplant. It'll break his heart. That's probably what happened with this guy. Then, when he acts out, they blame the dog."

"The wrong dog for that neighborhood," I said. It was a reflex, from years of thinking about how some roses are roses and some are weeds and the only difference is where they are or when they're planted.

"Exactly!" Porter said. "He's not a freaking fern!"

Porter owned ten acres, but only a half-acre of it had the kind of fence you needed for a dog, especially a smart one like an Aussie. The rest of what had once been a much larger ranch was open space, dotted with leaning fence posts, a abandoned stock tank, and a windmill that pumped water for the tank. The stock tank was meant for cattle. Now it served only deer.

He pointed to a small ramp that led down into the tank.

"I built that escape ramp so I wouldn't have to keep fishing drowned coyotes out of there before breakfast."

At the back of the property was a stand of old pine trees that looked as though they'd wandered down from the mountains and forgotten to go home.

All untouched and unplanned.

It was everything the Algorithms hated.

Porter grabbed some tools. "Gotta make sure the fence is coyote-proof," he said. He ran his hand along the fence as he walked. "Dogs inspect fences. Coyotes put them to the test."

He grinned.

"And the deer just don't care."

The path we walked had been cleared by years of dogs running along the fence line while deer and other free creatures taunted them from the other side.

Porter plunked one of the fence's wires to see if it was loose.

"Sounds almost like a banjo, doesn't it?" He pulled two wires at the same time, producing a sharp pizzicato chord.

"I'll be. It's a minor third. Like a French police siren." He sang the interval a few times as he plucked a few more wires in search of a major chord but found none.

It took us almost an hour to inspect the fence, although a lot of that time was spent looking at an impressively muscular buck and the three smaller females he was escorting across the open space.

"That's Henry." Porter looked like he was watching an old friend. "He's been coming here for years. And that's his family."

Porter declared the fence Banjo-ready. More importantly, it was coyote-ready.

"Let's go get our dog," he said.

Pa's Dog Rescue was the unofficial shelter of Elbert County—no sign, no website, just a barn full of strays and a clipboard. He started it after one of Porter's clients had a dog die. She left behind five orphaned beagle pups. Pa took them in and fed them formula with a Playtex glove, one hungry mouth on each finger.

Porter said Pa gave the first batch away for free. Then someone asked if he could take in an adult husky/wolf hybrid that was no longer a puppy. It wasn't long before the vet was asking if Pa could take in another rescue. Jill—Pa's wife—was the one who suggested asking for a small adoption fee to cover food. She also got the official license to run a kennel.

Porter got involved when another litter showed up needing round-the-clock feeding and Jill asked if he'd help out.

"We're not going to have to use a glove for this one, are we?" I asked.

"For Banjo?" Porter shook his head. "No. He's six months old. His mama would've cut him off a long time ago." He looked at me.

"You really don't know dogs, do you?"

Banjo's first night in Porter's house was, in a word, restless. Not in the "destroy your couch cushions" sense. I wondered if that had been beaten out of him by his previous owner. It was more of a "Are you sure this is where I'm supposed to be?" kind of edginess. The restlessness of uncertainty.

"He's just getting to know the place," Porter said. "Let him be."

Banjo paced from room to room, claws tapping quietly on the wood floor. He sniffed every corner, skirted around the kitchen table as if he was herding the chairs, and made a complete loop around the living room before circling back to Porter, who was sitting cross-legged on the rug watching his new roommate.

Porter patted the floor a few times to attract the dog's attention.

"Well, Banjo, this is your kingdom now," he told the dog. "Nothing to herd, but we'll see what we can do about that."

We set up the crate—the same crate that just a few hours before had held a Saint Bernard—in the corner of the living room. For a six-month-old Aussie, it was huge. The old blanket and toy sheep Pa brought with him didn't take up nearly enough room.

Banjo sniffed at the crate, circled once, and gave Porter a look that was equal parts suspicion and resignation.

Porter crouched down to look into the crate from Banjo's perspective. "I know. It's not exactly the Brown Palace, but it's the only crate I've got and I don't want you wandering around alone while I'm asleep." We arranged another blanket and a few towels inside to make it feel less like a cavern and more like a den.

Banjo stepped inside, turned twice, and faced the door as if he expected Porter to walk away forever. Porter latched the door gently, then sat on the floor, his legs crossed and his back against the couch next to the crate.

The dog let out a low, resigned whine. Then he laid his head on his paws and kept his eyes on Porter. I didn't want him to feel as if he was surrounded by strangers so I called it a night and went to bed.

I walked in the next morning to find Porter stretched out on the floor on a blanket, a few feet from the crate. Banjo was watching him from the other side of the door.

Banjo hesitated for only a second when Porter opened the crate. Then he stepped out and pressed his head against Porter's knee. Not quite trust, but maybe the start of it.

I patted him on the head and got ready for my walk with Biscuit.

10

By Friday, I was looking forward to my morning walk with Biscuit, which was something I hadn't felt about a job in a long time.

We finished our two laps, but I still hadn't seen my flower. Too many people and too many distractions for Biscuit. Churchill's slower pace gave me more time to look around. The basset hound moved in spurts. We'd be barely walking or not walking at all. Then he'd put his nose to the ground and start tracking something, straining at the leash and nearly pulling my arm out of its socket along the way.

As I approached the camera pole for the third time that morning, I braced myself for the reality that my flower might have been removed again, never to be seen. I wasn't going to lose to the Algorithm. I was losing to somebody with a pathological need for order.

Then I saw it.

And then I saw another one.

My flower was no longer alone. Someone—I had no idea who—had planted a bright red coneflower just a finger's width from mine. I had an unknown co-conspirator.

I wondered if the flower was from the older woman who'd nearly gotten wiped out by the skateboarder. She had the kind of healthy disdain for rules that might lead to non-compliance, but she also seemed genuinely frightened by what happened to Mr. Johnson and his rosebush. I doubted she had an extra $500 for a fine, or the strength to turn over a spade full of dirt.

It could have been any of the Regulars.

But there it stood. While my purple flower blended into the background, this one was blazing red.

This guy didn't just plant a flower. He planted a flag.

I took Churchill home and went back to Porter's to research potential employers. I revised my résumé for the tenth time and wrote a corresponding cover letter for each, all generated by AI. I was in search of the holy grail: the perfect mixture of boilerplate language with just enough empty spaces to make it employer specific.

But honestly, at that time, all I really wanted to do was walk dogs and check on my flower.

I went back to Tuttle's and headed straight to the coneflowers.

"Wow," Tuttle said. "Five plugs this time. You're really investing in your yard, aren't you?"

"Just trying to make the world a little better," I said.

It was getting dark by eight-thirty but the park stayed open until ten. I went back around nine, after it was dark and most of the people were gone. I was planning to plant one of my new flowers with the other two, so I only brought one with me.

But as my spade broke new ground, I realized it might be fun to plant the next flower a little further down the walking path.

I liked the idea of building a trail with a stranger.

I moved on to find the next belay, as it were, and hoped my anonymous partner would follow my lead.

"Let me get this straight." Porter said when I told him about my clandestine botanical activity later that night. "You're out there planting outlaw coneflowers in the dark like some kind of reverse crime fighter. Then this guy answers your call…"

"It wasn't really a 'call,'" I told him. "I didn't expect anyone to plant another flower. If anything, I thought they would be gone."

"Right." Porter scrunched up his face and stroked his chin. "Except it wasn't." He held up one finger and started pacing. "He finds your flower and joins your fight."

"Not really much of a fight," I said.

He stroked his chin. "This is no mere gardener, Wendell. No, no, my friend. This is a man—or a woman, you never know—on a mission. He's probably wanted to do this for years. You, my friend, have inspired him. You have given him permission to be what he's always wanted to be."

"I have been told I can be inspirational," I laughed.

"You are to him." Porter put both hands on the kitchen counter and pointed a finger at me.

"You've started a movement, you and your, your, your…" He seemed to be searching for the right word.

"Guerrilla gardening?" I offered.

Porter slammed both palms on the countertop. "Yes! Guerrilla gardening!"

"I'm not sure three flowers constitutes guerrilla gardening," I said.

Porter ignored me. "Who knows where this thing could lead?" He paced away but then spun around to face me.

"This is exactly the kind of spirit the Algorithms were designed to suppress!" he said. "They say it's about weeds or safety or even continuity, but it's really about maintaining the status quo. Control. Intimidation. Making people feel helpless until they just give up out of sheer exhaustion."

I bit my lip to keep a straight face.

"I really don't think…." I started saying.

"You're speaking flowers to power," Porter said. He shook his fist at the sky. "And the people will rise up, like…"

He turned and looked at me like an actor who'd forgotten his line.

"What are you planting?" he asked.

"Coneflowers," I said.

Porter continued with the fervor of a revival preacher.

"And the people will rise up, like coneflowers reaching for the sun!"

"Coneflowers don't really get that tall," I reminded him. "They're actually kind of small."

"Oh, yeah." He squinted as he nodded knowingly. "It starts small. That's why they're scared. They know. Today, it's coneflowers. Tomorrow, hollyhocks. Then a Giant Himalayan Lily!"

"I don't think a Himalayan Lily would survive in this climate," I said. "Giant or otherwise."

Porter spun around to face me.

"That's what they said about the Y chromosome, Wendell, and yet here we are."

The flower trail grew over the next week like a slow conversation between strangers. I'd plant a purple coneflower in the evening shadows, then return the next morning to find a red one standing beside it, with another red planted several yards ahead, my mystery partner's move in our botanical chess game. I'd answer with purple, advancing our silent conversation along the kale-lined pathway.

Some mornings brought surprises: a cluster of three reds where I'd expected one, or a single bloom placed daringly close to a security camera. The park was too busy and the flowers too obvious for no one to have seen them. I wondered if this was how the manzanita survived on El Capitan: hiding in plain sight, ignored by people who never realized it was there.

By the end of the week, we'd created a dotted line of rebellion stretching nearly half the length of one side the track—a coneflower trail of defiance that somehow made the whole park feel more alive.

11

I had no dogs scheduled for Saturday, but Banjo insisted on getting me up anyway. He barked at sunrise and barked louder every time I pretended not to hear.

"Banjo, seriously. What is it?" I muttered as I cracked open my bedroom door. In the living room, Porter stood transfixed, coffee mug in hand, eyes fixed on the sliding glass door. He only nodded when I said good morning.

Henry—the massive buck from yesterday—and three smaller deer were grazing inside the dog yard. Not out in the field but inside the smaller fence. The four deer were less than fifty feet from the sliding glass door that went into the kitchen.

"I thought fences were for keeping the animals out," I said.

Porter kneeled beside Banjo, his voice even. "It keeps out coyotes. Skunks. Raccoons. Things like that." He scratched Banjo's ears. "Deer don't care about fences, do they?"

"They jumped the fence?" I asked.

Porter made a broad swoosh with his arm. "Like they were pulling Santa's sleigh. You should have seen it."

I'd never seen a deer that big up close before. I glanced at Porter.

"There go your tomato plants," I told him.

"Oh well." He shrugged. "It's early in the season. I'll plant more."

"I can't believe they'd come right in your yard like that."

Porter raised one eyebrow. "They're probably thinking the same thing about us. This was their yard before it was mine."

"They're stealing your tomatoes," I reminded him.

"So did the neighbor's kids until I put up the fence," Porter said. "It's survival of the fittest."

I got the leash for Banjo.

"I was thinking of taking Banjo to the park for a walk," I told Porter. I really just wanted to check the flowers. Banjo was a convenient excuse to go.

"He'd love it." Porter dropped to Banjo's level and scratched his ears. "Wouldn't you?" he said to the dog. "Yes, you would."

Then he looked up at me with a very serious expression.

"Just don't let him off the leash—he'd go straight for the geese."

I was hopeful but not optimistic about what Banjo and I might find at the park. They mowed the grass at Farrier every Friday afternoon.

Our flowers were probably mulch by now. I explained all of this to Banjo on the drive over. He seemed to share my concerns.

Banjo's walk started the second I opened the car door. I tried to keep up.

Banjo didn't track like Churchill. Churchill kept his nose glued to the ground and looked up only to get his bearings. Banjo was more of a sampler than an investigator. He zigzagged across the parking lot, inhaling new smells with no indication of any interest in slowing down. I did my best to hang on and steer him toward the track. He calmed down only slightly once we hit the track and things became more predictable.

The fresh-cut grass was still covered in dew. I was afraid the flowers might have been mowed instead of pulled up. As we got closer, I prepared for the worst.

Then I saw our flowers.

Not only were coneflowers not mowed down, they stood out like flags on a putting green, surrounded by fresh-cut grass that matched the mowed grass on the rest of the green. Someone had intentionally mowed around them. Then they had gotten off the mower and trimmed the grass by hand.

Someone was working with us from the inside.

I walked to where I'd put my next flower. Same thing. The flower was still standing unharmed, surrounded by freshly cut grass.

I checked to see if any of The Regulars were watching. They weren't. They probably couldn't see that far.

Seated near the Regulars and looking like every real estate agent who ever appeared on a bus bench was my brother, Ben.

As soon as I saw him, I knew I was trapped. Turning around meant facing skateboarders head on and other safety compliance violations.

I bent down to tie my shoe and hoped Ben hadn't seen me. Then I saw him walking over anyway.

"Nice to see you, Wendell," he said from about thirty feet away. "Leonard told me I might find you here."

"I didn't realize Mr. Bixely was keeping up with me," I said. I wondered what else Leonard might know. And what he had told my brother.

"I ran into him on the golf course," Ben explained. "He says hello, by the way."

Banjo sniffed Ben's shoes and walked in a circle around him, herding in slow motion and wrapping his leash around Ben's ankles. I resisted the urge to pull.

"I would love to stand here and chat," I said, "but I have to get Banjo back home."

"No problem," Ben said as he tried to step over Banjo's leash. "I'll walk to your car with you." I helped Ben free himself from the leash.

My brother and I never had what you could really call a "talkative" relationship. We got along just fine, as brothers go. We just never said anything.

As an adult, I realized our silence may have been what sustained our relationship.

Ben broke that silence.

"Leonard tells me you broke up with Angela," he said.

"*Wow*," I thought. "*Did not see that coming.*"

"A couple of months ago, yeah."

"I thought she was the one," he said.

"I did too," I told him. "I guess I was wrong. These things happen."

"Do you know why," he asked, "or was it just one of those things?"

I knew why. And I knew I didn't want to share.

"It just didn't work out, Ben. That's all." I patted him on the shoulder. "But thank you so much for caring enough to ask."

"I take it you don't want to talk about it," he said.

"I really don't." I pulled Banjo toward me and tried to put him between Ben and me.

"It's done," I said. "Let's just leave it at that."

"He also told me you'd quit your job."

"Who knew Leonard was such an information hub?" I said. "He's right. I did."

He stopped walking.

"You OK?" Ben asked. "What's going on?"

"Me?" I said. "Nothing's going on. I'm great. I've got a job I love. I'm getting more exercise than I've ever had in my life. And I spend my days with dogs instead of people. I'm good."

"Please tell me this wasn't part of some political statement on your part. Some kind of protest thing."

"It really wasn't," I told him. I wanted to add, "*But that was before I became a guerilla gardener*," but decided not to reveal my secret identity.

"Your job was important," he assured me. "What you did mattered."

"You think stopping people from planting fescue instead of Kentucky bluegrass is life changing work?" I asked.

The morning sun made my car shine like an oasis across the parking lot. I allowed Banjo to pick up the pace.

"I'd love to stay and chat," I told Ben, "but I won't. Say hi to Mom for me."

I thought about Angela while I drove home. I met her during my first year as a Compliance Officer, when I was validating a landscape compliance complaint at the school where she still teaches. That was the process: Someone would report an incident or we'd see something on a camera. An officer would be sent to see if an actual violation had occurred. We'd tried a fully automated system like they use for traffic lights, but we ended up dismissing a lot of cases and it was, honestly, embarrassing for the department and the Algos.

I suggested sending someone to visually inspect the complaints before we sent out notifications. Leonard agreed and told me that special someone would be me.

Which is how I ended up taking pictures of goldenrods outside a sixth-grade classroom window when the school secretary stepped up and told me she was going to call the police if I didn't leave.

"Are you responsible for these flowers?" I asked her.

"Me?" she said. "No. And what are you doing here?"

I explained who I was and asked who was responsible for the violation.

She walked me to Angela's classroom and sent her out to talk to me.

I found myself wishing we were meeting under different circumstances.

"Are you responsible for the flowers outside?" I asked, as if that was my best pickup line.

"The *Solidago*?" She smiled. "I'm sorry. Did you mean the goldenrods? They're a native species, they attract pollinators, and, not that it matters to someone like you, they're beautiful."

"*Solidago humilis*." I said, hoping to impress her with my own knowledge of Latin plant names. "They are a Section 4 invasive plant and a Level 2 allergen," I said.

"That's a myth," she said. "Goldenrod pollen is spread by animals, not by air. You wouldn't inhale this unless you rubbed your nose in it."

I brushed some pollen from my hands, but my fingers were still yellow.

"And they constitute an Algorithmic Landscaping Violation," I said.

Her jaw dropped.

"You're kidding me," she said.

"I am not," I said. "You cannot have level 2 allergens that close to a public building."

"Let me show you," she said. She took my hand and rubbed it on my face. "See? Now you're going to sneeze."

"Which proves my point," I said, noticeably without sneezing.

"No it doesn't," she said. Then she smiled. "If this was airborne, you'd already be sneezing."

I gave her a warning—a rarity among compliance officers—and told her I'd be back tomorrow to check to see if the flowers had been removed. She suggested I come back when the kids were at recess.

"We can talk then," she said.

"The flowers are still there," I told her the next day.

"And you're still not sneezing," she said. "And your eyes actually look less bloodshot than they were when I met you." She smiled. "I'm going to guess that's because yesterday was a Monday."

"I'm not trying to be a jerk…" I said. "But…"

"Then don't be." She pointed to her face. "See this? This is me not being a jerk. It's not that hard. Part of my job is to teach kids how not to be a jerk."

"But," I continued, "those flowers are an Algorithmic Landscaping Violation. We take those seriously."

"And that means I have to take them seriously?" she asked.

"You should," I said.

She laughed. "I'm sorry. I just can't."

I still didn't write her a ticket.

We met again, completely by accident, in Farrier Park. She was looking at the goldenrods in their goldenrod flowerbed.

"Nice *Solidago*," I said, saying the word as if it were an Italian music term.

"I thought these were evil incarnate," she said.

"These are in a controlled environment where they won't take over the park," I told her.

She took a step closer. "Explain to me how you control pollinators."

"You're a sixth grade teacher," I said. "Are you seriously asking me to explain the birds and the bees to you?"

That was five years ago. Angela moved into my place six months after that. She planted goldenrod outside her classroom window the entire time she was living with me.

Porter was grilling something on the back porch when Banjo and I got home, the same back porch where we watched Henry and his friends eat tomato plants that morning. There were no deer, probably because of the hickory smoke coming off the grill and the sudden absence of tomato plants.

I unleashed Banjo and watched him bolt out the backdoor in search of deer that were long gone.

I kept my distance from the smoke and watched from inside the kitchen. The "Carbon Neutral Chef"—proclaimed as such by the BBQ apron he was wearing—had four bright red, one-and-a-half inch thick steaks on the grill. Smaller portions waited on a tray for their turn on the fire.

The chef pointed to a bench that I could have sworn was not there yesterday.

"Have a seat," he offered. "Tell me what you think."

"Nice." I rubbed my hand along the back of the bench. "Where did this come from?"

"In front of the courthouse," he said. "The leg was split. It was a hazard, Wendell. I'm saving lives here."

"You stole a broken bench from the courthouse?"

"I'm fixing a broken bench," Porter said. "If I hadn't taken it, they'd file a work order, wait for the repair guy over there to fix it, and then replace the whole bench six months later after he didn't get around to it."

He stopped and looked at me.

"How does he even have a job?" Porter asked, as if I knew. "Anyway, I figured I'd just fix the part that's broken and take it back tomorrow."

He waved his spatula. "Grab a plate," he said. "These are almost ready."

I went to the cabinet.

"You have really stepped up your culinary game," I told him. In my life, tuna steaks were extremely rare, as in "rarely made an appearance." When they did, I enjoyed a cool center.

I held out my plate and approached the chef, salivating with every step.

"Here you go!" Porter turned.

"Wait," I said. "I thought that was tuna. What is that?"

"Grilled watermelon," he beamed. "It's grrrrreat!" Porter carefully placed the red slab on my plate. "Next up, grilled cantaloupe!"

"You can't grill watermelon," I argued, despite holding clear evidence that one could, indeed, have a watermelon barbeque.

"Not true," Porter said. "That's a lie spread by Big Beef." He flipped one of the watermelon slices over and admired the grill lines against the fruity red flesh.

"This is the good stuff."

12

I let Porter's faux tuna dissolve on my tongue while I thought about what to do with my life. Dog walking was nice, but it was a side gig at best. It had been almost two weeks since I quit my job. Porter had been great, but I didn't want to stay there forever.

"You won't be happy in a new job until you understand why you quit your old one," he said. "So, why'd you quit?"

"I don't know," I said. "Why'd you quit what you were doing before you started doing whatever it is you call what you do now?"

He raised his eyebrows and looked very proper.

"The term you're searching for is 'professional pet care provider.'"

"Yeah," I said. "That. You didn't go to college to do that."

"Don't remind me," he laughed. "I could have saved a lot of money." He closed his eyes as he chewed a piece of cantaloupe. "But then I would not be the magnificent self-made man you see before you today."

He popped another piece of the grilled melon into his mouth.

"I wonder how this would work if you put this on rice with a little seaweed band around it?" he said.

"Nigiri cantaloupe?" I said.

"Yeah!" he said. "Faux sake nigiri!."

"You were saying," I reminded him. "How did you get from there to here?"

"I was a firefighter. You know, the guys with the sexy calendars?" He did a Hulk-style muscle flex.

"I remember when you started doing that," I said. Neither one of us wanted to say it out loud, but we'd drifted apart once Porter became a firefighter. Life happened. But he was still there when I needed him.

"But what happened after that?" I asked.

"I retired early," he said. "Just couldn't do it anymore."

My mind filled with horrible images of what a firefighter might witness on the job.

"Did you see something horrible? Is that why you quit?"

"Oh yeah," he said. "Plenty of crispy critters." He looked at me. "That job really makes you appreciate life. And it seriously warps your sense of humor." He used his chopsticks to pick up another piece of faux salmon cantaloupe. "But that's not why I quit. I quit because of tinnitus."

"Tinnitus? You still have that?" He'd told me about this years ago. I didn't realize it never went away.

"Oh, yeah. Horrible. I have this constant f-sharp, right up in the piccolo range, in my right ear. Songs in the key of G are painful." He shuddered. "The dissonance."

"You're serious."

"Why would I lie about that? You learn to live with it, like you live with the fridge or the buzz of electric lights. And it's gotten better since I left. But it still spikes when there's a loud noise."

He stared across the back yard.

"I do miss the silence, though." He started to put his plate in the sink. It was my turn to do dishes.

"I loved that job," he said. "But that's why I quit. The sirens, the alarms, the bells—those are bad enough, but once this started, they'd trigger the piccolo inside my head and it would just get louder. Like it was demanding to be heard or something."

He shuddered from his wrists to his ankles.

"Makes you understand why firetrucks carry deaf dalmatians," he said.

"And you started walking dogs after that?" I asked.

"Around then, yeah," he said. "I guess I missed the dalmatian we had at the station. So I started walking other people's dogs."

I thought about what Porter said about not getting a new job until I knew why I'd quit my old one. I didn't quit because of the job, although that would have been reason enough. Nobody grows up pretending to be a compliance officer.

I wish I could say I'd considered my life choices and couldn't take another day of giving old people tickets for rosebushes, but my reasoning wasn't that noble.

I quit because of Leonard.

I thought about seeing what might be available in Algorithmic Language Compliance, but I felt less comfortable telling people what they couldn't say than I did about telling them to get rid of their shrubbery.

House Color Compliance never had any turnover. No open slots there.

I called a friend in Algorithmic Recreational Equipment Compliance.

"Leonard told us to expect your call," he said.

"Us?" I asked. "Is there more than one supervisor for Rec Compliance?"

"No," he said. "Us as in all the supervisors. Said you weren't a team player. Gotta say, quitting with no notice like that does not look good."

"Does it not look good, or is it highly frowned upon?" I asked. I wasn't sure of the extent of my violation.

"You just don't do it," he said.

"So much for my inside connections," I thought. No worries. Risk management is a huge field that applies to everything. Especially money. I'd find another job.

I was in the process of filling out an online application for one of the big investment firms in downtown Denver when a chat window opened up at the bottom of my screen.

"Hello. I'm Ralph, your virtual career liaison. How may I help you?"

"Let me speak to a human," I typed.

"Are you sure? I would be glad to answer any question you might have."

I copied and pasted my original request.

"Are you sure?" said the AI.

"Yes!" I slammed on the keyboard. "Just let me speak to a human!"

"One moment please."

I'm not sure what level "human" I was being connected to, but I was determined to make a good impression.

"Hi. I'm Wendell Jones," I typed. "I have five years in risk management. I'm considering a change of scenery and wondered if we might talk."

"Where are you currently working?" came the reply.

"Just left my position as Algorithmic Landscape Compliance Officer with Peregrine Perch."

The laughter emoji erased any suspicion I may have had about whether I was talking to a human or to AI.

"So, you managed the risk of daisies?" said the text.

"Rogue daisies," I corrected him. As if that made a difference. "But yeah. That was pretty much it. I like to think I was enforcing the aesthetic standards of a meticulously planned community."

"You realize we manage risk for firms with billions of dollars in potential liabilities, right?"

"That's a lot of daisies," I said.

"Yes it is," typed the human who by this time was probably wishing he was AI. Or that I was.

"Good luck with your job search."

Very polite. Very professional. And very Algorithmic, even if he was a human.

"You know," I told Porter over leftover watermelon, "I've been to Tuttle's a lot lately. I don't think I've seen anyone in there besides him. Does he have any help?"

"Ray?" Porter asked. "I think he did. But I also hear he's pretty picky about who waters his lettuce."

I drove over to talk to Mr. Tuttle.

"Back for more coneflowers?" he asked.

I walked up to his counter empty handed. He brushed some potting soil from the counter.

He pointed a spade at me. "Now I know where I've seen you. Aren't you that compliance guy? Algorithm Landscape Compliance?"

"I am," I confessed. "Or I was until recently."

"Why'd you quit?" he asked.

"Because I was tired of telling people what they couldn't plant." It wasn't a complete answer, but it was honest as far as it went.

And it went far enough for Mr. Tuttle.

"I hate the Algorithms," he said flatly. "I had to relocate my nursery because they wouldn't let me sell noncompliant plants. Had a nice place on Main Street in Peregrine Pearch. Ended up out here."

"So you thought it would be easier to move than to get rid of the plants?" I asked.

"It would have been easier if I had stayed," he said. "But not all of my customers live in the Perch. I've got customers from at least four counties around here. And not just backyard gardeners. I've got contractors, developers, contracts with some of the cities."

Tuttle looked at the open sky and the open, rolling view from his parking lot. There was a genuine affection there.

"But it worked out," he said. "Ended up being a good thing."

"Then you know how I feel," I said.

"No, I don't know how I feel," he stated flatly. "You went around the Perch for years, forcing people to pull up plants that made them perfectly happy. Not weeds, mind you. Just plants that happened to be in the wrong place or were one flower over the quota." He paused and took a deep breath.

"Landscaping is an art," he said, "right up there with Monet, Picasso, or Rodin. People like you turned it into a paint-by-numbers chart with a beige background."

He smiled like he'd caught me in a trap. "So you quit your job and now you're here. Are you looking for some absolution or something?"

"I've had a change of heart," I told him. "But, I can use what I learned over there to help you now."

Tuttle did not look impressed. "How?"

"I know the Algorithms like I know *Buxus sempervirens* or *Syringa vulgaris.*"

The older man was not impressed. "We don't really speak much Latin here," he said. "How's your Spanish?"

"Boxwoods and Lilacs," I said. I'm sure I sounded like the smug bureaucrat I was. It's hard to drop the accent or the attitude.

"I said we don't speak much Latin," Tuttle said. "I didn't say we didn't know our plants." He gave me a moment to fully appreciate the heat that was rising in my cheeks.

"And how is all this esoteric knowledge supposed to help me?" he asked. "I mean, that is what you're doing, right? Looking for a job?"

"Yes, I am," I said. "I could steer people away from plants that are non-compliant and save them a violation."

Tuttle laughed. "You think the people that buy those plants don't know they're committing a violation?"

"Fair enough," I said. "I could show them how they can use the ratio charts to know which plants are expected to be restricted by ratios next year. Let them get theirs in the ground first. Beat the quota."

"Again," Tuttle asked, "do you think people who do that really care about your ratios?"

"Some might," I said. "Especially if they're repeat offenders who can't afford to get in trouble."

He looked at his watch.

"I don't need an Algorithm Landscape Compliance Officer." He looked at the empty space in front of the Employee Parking sign.

"I need somebody who'll show up for work on time," he said. "Show up on time, water the plants, and help unload the truck on Tuesdays. That's the job."

He looked me in the eye.

"Can you do that?"

"I can."

"Then you're hired. Come in Monday. We open at nine. Be sure you're here when we do."

13

I woke up to Banjo barking at the same four deer that had him barking the day before.

I put the backpack with two coneflower plugs into the back of my car, one to answer the latest red flower and the other for the next stop along the trail.

"Banjo, let's go for a walk."

I was juggling the backpack and Banjo's leash when I saw Erica and Biscuit crossing the street. I put the backpack back in the car. The dogs would be the only ones to do any trail marking today.

Erica looked at me and smiled. "Susan told me," she said.

I tried to think of any Susans I might have known and what they might feel the need to tell Erica.

"So you know?" I said.

"I know about when you tried to shove a noncompliant bag into the receptacle," she said. "And that you nearly broke the lid and did this weird squinty grimace face thing looking straight into the camera. She sent that picture to me. Your face is now on my desktop."

I breathed a hopefully undetected sigh of relief.

"And you didn't say anything?" I asked.

"Why would I? You were walking my dog. She recognized Biscuit and asked me if my dog was missing. I was impressed you thought to bring some bags with you. I'm especially impressed that you carried it for another half a mile before you could get rid of it."

"It seemed like the right thing to do," I told her.

Erica stopped cold.

"There." She pointed ahead and walked over to the first two flowers on our trail.

She spun around with a huge smile.

"Susan also told me about this flower she saw while she was walking her dog. Just a single flower in the grass by itself. I told her I didn't think the Algos would allow an individual flower like that. But then she saw it again the next day. And then another one. And I guess someone else planted a red one beside the purple one that was already there."

"It's a conspiracy." I joked. "A conspiracy against the Algorithms."

I turned to my dog.

"Come on, Banjo," I said, as I tugged on the leash to pull him closer to me.

"And they're doing this kind of leapfrog thing, planting flowers." Erica laughed. Biscuit turned to look at her.

She kneeled down and touched the flowers like she was handling fine lace. Then she looked up at me and blushed just enough to make her cheeks pink.

"Sometimes I picture him," she said.

"Who?"

"This mystery gardener." She looked up at me. "The one who's doing this."

I didn't say anything. I tried to make sure my face didn't either.

A part of me wanted to say "you're welcome" or something. It felt good to be appreciated, even if she didn't know it was me. There was also the part of me that didn't want to be seen at all. Not by the Regulars. Certainly not by Leonard. Not by anyone. Westley doesn't tell Buttercup he's the Dread Pirate Roberts until the third act.

She cocked her head to one side and looked at the flowers as she spoke.

"He's older, I think. Not old-old, but like... seasoned. Wears boots even when it's hot." She smiled at the image. "Probably has dirt under his fingernails he can't scrub out. Plants things in the dark and walks away before anyone sees. But then—here's the weird part—I imagine him watching to see who stops. Just standing there with a thermos of chamomile tea, waiting to see if the flowers survive."

Biscuit sat. Banjo chewed on a stick.

"I think he smiles when people stop and look." She looked back at me again, to make sure I had the image. "Especially the ones who pretend not to. The joggers. The Regulars. The tai chi crowd. They look. They just won't admit it."

I don't own a pair of boots. I don't drink chamomile tea. And I wasn't sure where I landed along the old to old-old spectrum. Can you be young-old?

"I'm sure his mother's proud," I said.

"She should be," Erica said. "This guy's doing something good. Something kind. And a little reckless. You don't get a lot of that anymore."

She stood up and brushed the mulch off her knees.

"I like thinking he's out there," she said. "Whoever he is."

I liked the idea of some Sam Elliott character out there with dirt under his nails and chicken soup in his thermos. I could hear him saying "The Gardener Abides." But you can't be anonymous and applauded at the same time. That's the deal.

"But that's only one of them," I reminded her. "Somebody is answering with flowers of their own. What about them?"

Erica smiled like she was imagining the possibilities.

"She doesn't know who he is," she speculated. "Maybe she's seen him from a distance, but they've never met. And he's never seen her."

"That makes sense," I wondered if my mystery partner had seen me from somewhere behind the bushes. I knew nothing about them. What did they know about me?

I changed the topic before I accidentally revealed my secret identity.

"You're in Compliance," I reminded her. "You must know the danger of allowing someone to do something like that."

"I'm in Algorithmic Seasonal Decoration Compliance," she said.

I froze. Banjo almost pulled me over before he stopped.

"You're *that* Erica?" I had to ask. "The one who made that family take down that two-story tall inflatable Darth Vader Santa thing? What did the Algorithm notice say?"

I did my best to remember the line, the wording was so perfect.

Erica proudly recited the notification: "This structure exceeds neighborhood quotas for tall seasonal décor and promotes an anti-business message. Please remove within five days."

My breath stopped mid-inhale, I was so impressed with the eloquence of it all. Biscuit looked concerned and came to my side.

"Yeah," she said. "The Algorithm does not allow anti-business messaging or anything that might be construed as anti-commerce."

"You are legend."

She blushed a little. "Ah, thank you so much. It's not that exciting most of the time." She looked for our next group of flowers.

"I don't care what the Algorithm allows," she said while she searched. "It's nice to see something that wasn't planned. And if it really is wild and wasn't paid for somewhere, then even better."

We followed the flower trail as far as it went. I said something about how I guessed that was as far as the flower planters got.

"Well, I hope they keep going," she said. "I hope they win."

"Win what?" I really wanted to know what people had heard.

"I don't know," she said. "Whatever it was they wanted to win when they started planting those flowers."

Banjo and I went back home. I could see Henry and his female entourage through the back door when we came in, munching on grass in the rear of the fenced-in backyard. It was early enough that Porter left the sliding glass door open to let in some fresh air while he stirred Greek yogurt into his coffee.

Banjo saw the small herd and sprang into action. He bolted across the living room, into the kitchen, and out the open door toward the deer. Porter stepped out on to the patio like he had seen a hummingbird and wanted a closer look.

"That's not good," Porter said. He took another sip of coffee. "But, there's nothing we can do about it. Let's watch the show."

I expected Banjo to run straight at the small herd. Instead, he trotted toward the opposite side of the yard. He didn't bark, didn't lunge, didn't charge. He moved away from the four deer, purposeful but not fast enough to spook Henry or the sister-wives. Then he curved North, gradually tightening his arc to approach the weakest of the herd, a smallish doe that brought up the rear.

Banjo's ears pointed forward as he tightened the arc, his head low and his tail level with his back like a wolf. He seemed to understand that if he didn't panic, the deer wouldn't panic either. At least not right away.

The deer clustered near the fence. Banjo kept the pressure up, never too much, just enough to keep them from splitting. When a doe tried to break away, Banjo ran ahead of her and brought her back. The dog was creating order out of wildness, like he'd been waiting his whole life for this exact moment.

In his world, Banjo was the Algorithm.

Henry decided to jump the fence to freedom. He moved toward the center of the yard, where he would have enough of a runway to clear the six-foot hurdle. Banjo cut the big buck off as he ran, dancing around and between his front legs and antlers like a gymnast. He refused to let Henry get more than five or six feet away from the fence; certainly not the fifteen feet or more of runway that he'd need to clear it.

"I thought you said he wasn't trained," I said.

"He's not." Porter sounded almost reverent. "That's pure instinct."

The smallest doe ran and jumped but ended up crashing chest-first into the fence, front legs splayed out like she was waiting for a pat down.

The big buck broke away and ran toward the back fence. The three smaller deer tried to keep up. Banjo raced ahead, cutting off the stampede and edging them back to where he wanted them to go.

That's when I saw where Banjo was moving them toward. The only gate in the yard: The open back door.

"That's not good," Porter observed.

"What's the command?" I asked Porter. "Quick! What did that farmer say when that dog herded those kids?"

"That'll do," Porter said quietly. He took a sip from his mug.

"Banjo!" I yelled. "That'll do!"

Porter blinked and stepped back closer to the house.

"The dog hasn't been trained," he reminded me. "You might as well tell him to have a nice day."

He got up to close the door, but he was too late.

The biggest doe bolted through the open sliding glass door and on to the kitchen table. She slid sideways, legs going all directions, hit the chair, bounced off, and shot into the living room.

The others piled up behind her. Henry stood in quiet dignity in the kitchen. Then he proceeded to attack the couch.

Banjo followed at full gallop, proud as a kindergartner who just learned to tie his shoes and wants to do it for everyone, everywhere, forever.

Porter's mouth dropped open when the table collapsed beneath the weight of the third deer. He kept looking back and forth, between the front door and the carnage happening in his living room.

I watched Porter process the destroyed furniture, the chaos, the disruption of his peaceful life. His face tensed for just a moment. Then he slowly nodded his head, took a deep breath, and pulled out his phone.

"Man," he said. "I have to get this."

Hooves and antlers flew, destroying anything in their path. The couch, the TV screen, and a lamp were destroyed. Porter raised his phone to get a better shot while he tried to avoid the bodies—deer and dog— that were flying around the room.

"Banjo!" I called. "Come here!"

Banjo ignored me. He was still trying to herd the truly wild deer into a circle. Henry thrashed his antlers, breaking shelves and shattering picture frames. He managed to put three holes in the sheetrock.

Porter picked the dog up from behind, held on to him despite his twisting, pawing, and thrashing, and deposited him in the nearest room, which happened to be the room where I was staying. Then he slid down the wall to the floor and continued to record the destruction of his home.

Porter kept recording until the deer were relatively calm. Then he got up, turned off all the lights, closed the drapes, and opened the front door—the deer equivalent of an emergency exit.

The big buck saw the light and ran toward it, smashing his antlers against the door frame for one final assault on the house. He turned his head to the side, worked his way through, and then ran across the front yard. The others followed close behind. Porter's home was calm once again.

We surveyed the damage. I've never been in a tornado, but they could not possibly be any worse than what was in that house that day.

"That was incredible!" Porter's hands spread wide as he shook his head in disbelief. "Banjo is a natural! Man, I've got to tell Pa about that. Somebody's going to love that dog!"

I picked up the broken table legs. Porter took shattered picture frames from the wall and even more from the floor. I watched as he carefully picked broken glass from a picture of a much younger him on what looked like a camping trip. He stopped to look at the picture once all the glass was removed.

"You okay?" I asked.

"Nothing that wasn't already broken," he told me.

That's when I saw something of my own that was broken on the floor.

I had put most of my furniture and other belongings in storage when I moved in with Porter. There just wasn't room in his place for another houseful of furniture. Angela took her things with her, along with our couch and a few other items we shared.

One thing Angela did not take was the rosemary plant she'd given me on our first Christmas together. It was shaped like a Christmas tree at the time, with some tiny ornaments she'd made with beads, a red ribbon, and a little silver star on top. She'd even wrapped up a few matchboxes to look like presents under the tree.

I'd kept that rosemary alive for four years. Angela was packing up to leave when I asked her if she wanted it back.

"No," she said. "That's yours."

I kept it. It reminded me of Angela, especially the smell. I would still break off rosemary leaves to sniff. They smelled like a forest after a thunderstorm. Then I'd crush the needles between my fingers, releasing a woody, lemony scent that brought back more memories than any picture.

My room didn't have the kind of light it needed, so I'd put it in the living room where it could get more sun. It no longer resembled a Christmas tree. It was more like an unkempt, bushy shrub in a pot with a few brown spots. Porter had been breaking off leaves when he wanted fresh rosemary for cooking.

After the stampede, dirt spilled out of the broken terracotta pot and all over the floor. Most of the stems themselves—rosemary doesn't have a single trunk but sends up several stems that thicken over time— were broken. Only two remained intact.

"Another casualty?" Porter asked.

"Afraid so," I said. "Not a big deal."

"We're lucky we didn't get hurt," Porter told me. "Look at this." He pulled out his phone to show me the video. Neither of us realized how many times we had to duck, dive, or dodge to avoid being hit by a deer. I also hadn't realized that Banjo was doing his best to get them to turn around and go back to the yard. That was before Porter put him in my room.

"I got the whole thing on video." Porter said. "Pa's going to want to see this."

14

It was almost dark before we'd swept up the broken glass so Banjo could come out of my room. Banjo surveyed the damage and sniffed every overturned item.

"Don't you dare say 'bad dog,'" Porter told me quietly. "He did exactly what he was born to do. You never want him to think herding is a bad thing or that he's going to get punished for working like that."

He kneeled beside Banjo and scratched him behind his ears. "Good boy. That's a good dog."

I can only aspire to Porter's level of serenity in the face of chaos.

My thoughts were preoccupied with the flowers that were still sitting in my backpack. They should be all right, but I wanted to plant them that night.

Porter and I divided things into two piles: Things that could be repaired and things that could not. The "things that cannot be repaired" pile was roughly twice the size of the pile of repairable items. Together, we put stuff that was just knocked out of place and did not need to be fixed back where it belonged.

Banjo showed his support by staying beneath our feet, right where we could trip over him.

We carried what had been destroyed to a large dumpster behind Porter's garage where it could stay until it was hauled away.

"I'm going to do my guerilla gardening thing before it's too late," I said. I felt guilty leaving, but I didn't want my mystery partner to think I'd abandoned them. "I'll help out when I get back. I just don't want this other guy to think I've given up."

"No problem. There'll be plenty left when you get back." Porter sat on the kitchen counter, eating an apple that somehow managed to escape the deer's attention.

I grabbed my backpack, put Banjo on his leash so he'd be out of Porter's way, and headed for the park. I spotted the red flower from about forty feet away.

"I see your flower..." I said to my absent accomplice after wrapping Banjo's leash around a bench leg. "And I raise you one more."

Then I saw the red and blue lights.

The police car was driving on the track, like a slow motion pace car that no one was following. I set my coneflower plugs on the ground and pretended to tie my shoes. Banjo huddled beneath my leg.

The car's headlights were in my face when I looked up. Despite my defiance of Algorithmic protocols, this was my first encounter with the actual Peregrine Perch PD.

The cruiser rolled to a stop a few yards away. The driver's window slid down with a mechanical whirr. I squinted into the beam of the spotlight and prepared to explain… something. Anything.

"Evening," the officer said from his car.

His voice was calm. A little bored, maybe. He sounded like someone nearing the end of his shift and hoping not to have to file paperwork.

"Evening," I said, still crouched like a man tying an endless knot in his sneakers.

The officer moved his floodlight back and forth and let the silence hang. He paused on the flowers but didn't say anything about them. I was temporarily blinded by the light, but I thought I saw him smile before he moved on.

Theoretically, the police department and the Algorithm Compliance Office both worked for the City of Peregrine Perch. In reality, the police routinely ignored Compliance violations, claiming that they were a civil, not criminal matter.

I learned of this interdepartmental friction early in my time in Compliance, when Leonard was away and I documented a flagrant landscape violation: two lawn gnomes and a giant ceramic frog, all sitting around a campfire of bright orange, red, and yellow tulips. It was all very whimsical. And it was a violation.

The "campfire" might have snuck by had it been made of junipers or boxwoods. But the Algorithms required all plants visible from the street to have "year-round visual consistency." According to the Algos, this made tulips a weed.

The Lawn Décor Compliance Office objected to the gnomes and the giant frog as "oversized decorative figures" and on the grounds of general good taste.

"Call us when there's a real crime," the officer told me when he met me at the address. "And remind Leonard that we don't work for him." This, of course, contradicted everything Leonard had said about how Algorithm Code Enforcement was the most respected of all city departments.

"Park'll be closing soon," was all he said, although I never understood how you close a park with no fence. Then he nodded, gave me the two-finger small town wave, and pulled away without another word.

I exhaled. Banjo tucked in closer to my knee.

Once the floodlight was gone and I could see again, I noticed a new red flower planted a few feet ahead.

I veered toward it, thinking I'd respond in kind. That's when I saw the scroll—plain white paper, rolled tight and tied with a red ribbon. A red coneflower was tucked under the bow like a wax seal.

I froze. My first thought wasn't curiosity or wonder or awe.

It was a fear of entrapment.

I fought the urge to read it right there. If it was an unfiltered human message—handwritten, no less—I didn't want to be caught holding it. Under Algorithmic Language Protocol, even failing to report that kind of thing could get you a violation notice. Depending on the wording, it might even be classified as subversive literature, although the definition of "subversive" seemed to be getting more inclusive with every Algorithm update.

I slipped the scroll into my backpack and planted both coneflowers where it had been so he'd know the scroll was safe.

Banjo and I cut across the middle of the park so I could get to my car and get home faster. I wanted to read my partner's note. Possibilities ran through my mind all along the fifteen minute drive. A spy? Some dark, foreboding warning that my life was being monitored in ways I could not begin to understand?

"I could use a little romance, Banjo," I said as I drove home. "Think that's it?"

With no place to really sit in the living room, I went to my bedroom to read. I broke the seal on the scroll and untied the ribbon.

There were three pages.

15

Dear Sarah,

I want to tell you how proud I was of you at the concert!

Your beautiful voice reminded me of how your mom sang when she was your age. Your grandmother would have loved it.

Thank you for reminding me to be there. I would never want to miss anything you do, but sometimes I forget. I am so glad I went.

I love you very much. Keep singing!

Love,

Grandpa

I didn't know how to react. I felt like I was intruding on a private moment. Why would a grandfather share such a personal letter with a complete stranger?

The second page was not handwritten. With Sarah's name and the date at the top of the page, it looked like a homework assignment that someone printed out.

Dear Grandpa,

Thank you for coming to our concert! I was so nervous before we started! Then I saw you and felt better. You probably felt like I was staring at you the whole time, especially during my solo. I don't think I could have sung that without seeing you there.

That's why I looked at you the whole time. I hope that was okay.

I love you,

Sarah.

I thought about Angela and how, as a sixth-grade teacher, she went to every school concert her students ever did. I went to a few. Middle school concerts aren't really my thing. Her students always giggled when they saw us together.

"Miss Teague, is he your boyfriend?" they'd tease. Or they may have been sincere. It's hard to tell with middle school kids.

"Well," Angela would say, "He's a boy. And he is my friend. So, I guess that makes him my boy friend." She emphasizing the space between the words with her eyes and a smile. Then she'd smile at me and the kids would put their hands over their mouths and scream and laugh before they ran away.

The third page was a copy of an Algorithmic Language Violation Notification.

"Your document, 'Letter to Grandpa', contains non-AI content and is therefore out of compliance with Algorithmic Language Compliance Code, Section 270-2, (b), "Personal correspondence."

Total Fine for first offense: $25

I gulped hard. I'd seen this before. Only the case number was different.

When I was living in the Perch with Angela—before El Capitan, before I quit my job—she showed me one of these. One of her sixth graders had turned in a homework assignment with completely original human writing. No AI whatsoever.

The Algorithm flagged it for containing "unverified human content." The student's original writing triggered a violation.

As a teacher and a mandated reporter of such things, Angela was required to confirm whether the student had written it or if someone else had helped. A parent, a tutor, another student. It didn't matter. If it didn't look like it was written by AI, if the computer determined that it hadn't been written by AI, it had to be reported.

What made this response especially egregious was that the assignment—generated by the Algorithms as part of the larger Algorithm curriculum—was "to use AI tools in personal correspondence." The whole point of the assignment was to teach students to use AI instead of their own words. "Self-expression through AI", the lesson plan said.

In Angela's report, she stated that an unknown party had accessed the keyboard—possibly a prank by another student.

"You lied to the Algos?" I asked.

"I tried to protect my student," she said. "But it didn't matter. The computer camera was still on, even if she wasn't using it."

"There are reasons for those protocols," I told her. "You've seen the research."

She just looked at me. "You've never broken a rule?"

"Of course not," I argued. "I follow the system."

"Even when you're writing something for me?"

"Especially then." I smiled. "That Valentine's Day card last year? The one that made you cry? Totally AI."

She moved out the next day.

That was four months ago. She picked up her stuff the next day, and I hadn't seen her since. Relationships were the one area that the Algos didn't touch. There were no Algorithms for human emotions. But there were Algorithms for communication, which is pretty much the same thing.

I thought about calling Angela to tell her I finally got it. I just didn't know how to say that. I was sure I shouldn't use AI for that message.

16

Erica was still wearing her bathrobe when I picked up Biscuit the next morning. She hid behind the door and smiled as she handed Biscuit's leash to me.

The seven AM crowd at Farrier Park was very different from the eight o'clock group. More joggers, more dog walkers. A tai chi class moved slowly in the center of the park—mostly retirees in pastel track suits, shifting their weight like Jello trying to remember how to stand up. I recognized some of them from the table by the pond. Others I didn't know, but I assumed they were Regulars who had swapped sitting for swaying. Other, presumably less flexible Regulars sat on benches under the pavilion. I could smell their coffee all the way to the track.

An older man with a gray beard that could have qualified for its own SeniorsOnly account sat alone at a chess table near the pond. I'd seen him before, always with the others, never apart like he was that morning. Either he was waiting for someone to join him or he was taking a break from entertaining the Regulars. Possibly both.

If he was there to play chess, he was missing a partner. If he was there for conversation, he'd overshot the mark by about fifty yards.

If he was there to let me know he'd left the scroll, he'd nailed it.

He was still there when Biscuit and I returned on our second lap. He looked at me like he knew something, which—given the scroll—he probably did. I had the strange feeling of being recognized for something I hadn't admitted doing.

I fought back the urge to think he might be some kind of undercover agent Leonard hired to get pictures of the Guerilla Gardner of Farrier Park.

I considered walking over, like in those movies where the cop on a stakeout gets made. Maybe ask, "Are you the one planting flowers and leaving scrolls?" But there wasn't a non-weird way to say it.

I nodded instead.

The landlocked Ancient Mariner made eye contact and nodded in return. I was sure he had to be the man who left the scroll. I just didn't know what to do with that information.

Erica was just pulling out of the driveway when Biscuit and I got back to her house. She stopped and put her window down.

"I was thinking," she said from inside her car, "if you're going to walk Biscuit this early, I could probably just walk him myself before work."

Biscuit turned and looked at me.

"I thought you didn't like getting up early," I said.

"I don't." She shrugged. "But I'll have to get up anyway if you're coming over to get Biscuit. All I'd have to do is throw on some sweats and go." We both knew that was a lie. Women like Erica do not simply "throw on some sweats" and leave the house, not even for a walk in the park. But I appreciated her willingness to get up early for me.

She opened the car door and stepped out.

"I don't usually see co-workers socially," she said.

"Not sure I qualify as a co-worker anymore," I told her.

"OK," she said. "Whatever you call this, you walking my dog. Me paying you." She brushed some hair away from her face. "But, if someone wasn't working for me, and I happened to see that someone out walking another dog in the park while I was walking Biscuit, then, I think, something might come from that."

"So you're telling me I'm fired," I said.

Erica's mouth dropped open and her eyes grew very wide.

"I had not thought of it that way," she said. "I know you're not doing this for your health. I will gladly pay you for this week."

"But," I said, "I don't usually take money from women I am seeing socially." I handed Biscuit's leash to her. "As it happens, I have accepted a position with a firm on the other side of town."

"A firm?" she said. "Sounds serious. Another compliance gig?"

"Tuttle's Nursery," I told her.

Her eyes lit up. "That's a great place. He's kind of grumpy, but he really knows his stuff."

"What would the Algos say about you walking with a former employee?"

She smiled. "I'm sure there's some ethical code about it somewhere, but, honestly, who cares? Think about it," she said. "Maybe we could get together sometime without the dogs." She looked at her phone for the time.

"Let's talk later," she said. "I've got to get to work before Leonard knows I'm late."

I put Biscuit in the house and headed back to Porter's. He was on the phone when I got home.

"So, if I'd lied, you'd cover it?" he was saying. "That's the policy?"

Porter was mid-argument, pausing only to mouth "Can you believe these guys?" in my direction. He went back to the call.

"All I said was the deer got in through an open door. I told the truth. So, if I'd made something up and said they knocked the door down, you'd pay for it? But because I was honest, I'm on the hook?" He tapped the screen a few times and tossed the phone onto the counter.

"I miss landlines," he said.

"I got a job," I told him. "I'll help cover the damages. Make up for some rent."

"Wendell." He stepped towards me. "I don't know if I'm ready for that kind of commitment. I haven't even met your parents."

"They're nice," I told him. "Retired. Live over near Morrison. Let me know what you decide about the furniture."

"I'll think about it, but no matching furniture."

I arrived at my new job a little before nine. Tuttle greeted me with a broom and a grunt.

"You're early." Tuttle put down his broom but kept the grunt. "That's a good thing. Come with me."

He led me out to the side lot where the Christmas trees lived four weeks a year. For the other forty-eight weeks, it was just a gravel bed for unsold pines and a few fruit trees waiting to be adopted. And occasionally a parking lot.

There, lying on a pallet, was an oak tree. It looked to be about fifteen feet long. The root ball was wrapped in wire and burlap. The tree looked like a fallen soldier from a more honorable war.

"Weighs just over a ton," Tuttle said.

"How do you even move a tree like that?" I asked.

"Hydraulic spade," Tuttle explained. "That's mostly for planting, but you can move it around in that if you have to."

He kept checking the tree for bird nests or other boarders.

"It's a shame, too," he said. "One day, it's a perfectly good tree. The next, someone decides they want to build something there and it suddenly becomes a very large weed. The city hired me remove to it for them. I can sell it, cut it up for firewood, whatever I want. It's not costing me anything but the drive over there."

"Is that a good deal?"

"If I can sell it, it will be," Tuttle said. "That tree's worth about two thousand dollars. There are landscaping contractors that would pay at least that much." He looked at me. "And if it doesn't sell, I can still get at least a two hundred dollars worth of firewood out of it."

He circled the tree again with a slow and thoughtful pace, like he was trying to see if anything was still living in it.

"Your job," he said, "is to keep her alive."

I flinched. Historically, I didn't have the best record with things referred to as "her."

"I'll do what I can," I told him.

"It's already dying," he said. "No matter what you do. You'll slow it down, maybe. But a month from now—at best—it's toast."

He handed me a hose and a drip line.

"Keep it damp, not soaked," he said. "Root rot's a thing. And make sure nothing moves in. A tree would make a nice place to live. I don't want to be showing it to some landscaper and have a raccoon family run out."

He was right. Even after Tuttle's careful inspection, I still found a baby rabbit under the pallets. I named him Jim. Jim ran off immediately. I respected that.

I finished my shift at six and had ninety minutes to kill before I was supposed to walk Churchill. I ran home, ate some form of leftover eggplant that Porter had in the fridge, and headed out again.

I took the manzanita plant with me.

I clipped Churchill's leash to a belt loop so I could carry the bonsai with both hands and retraced our steps to the spot where I'd found the scroll.

I dug the hole, then I carefully took the manzanita out of its ceramic pot and planted it. I didn't leave a note. Just the tree. My response to his scroll.

What had been a typically-sized bonsai suddenly looked very small in the context of Farrier Park. But its roots were free. Not that freedom guaranteed survival. Peregrine Perch wasn't known for great soil. But then again, neither was El Capitan.

I was still thinking about the manzanita when I got home. Porter met me at the door.

"The tree," he said. "It's gone."

"What tree?" I asked. I was thinking about the oak back at Tuttle's.

"The manzanita!" he said. "It's missing."

"I took it," I told him.

Porter stepped back like I'd hit him with a leaf blower.

"Did you take it to the nursery?" he asked. "Were you afraid it was going to die? Bonsai are hard. You should've said something. If it's a symbolic thing, I could've kept it for you. Watered it. Whispered encouraging things."

"I planted it," I told him.

"In the park?" he asked.

A grin broke across his face like sunlight over kale. "You, my friend, truly are the Guerilla Gardener. I am unworthy even to touch your trowel."

17

Erica and Biscuit met Banjo and me in the parking lot the next morning, just as the moon was calling it a night.

"I've been here since six-fifty," Erica said. "That was five minutes ago."

"So we agree that I'm early," I said.

She laughed. "I'm just saying I'm not usually outside this early."

Banjo tugged on his leash and reminded me that we were there to walk, not talk.

"Anything for the kids, right?" I said.

"Anything," she agreed.

We'd made it about thirty steps down the track when the calm Colorado sunrise was shattered by yipping puppies, screaming children, and the frantic cry of a woman chasing a pack of dachshund puppies on their first day away from mom. I counted eight, each with a colorful bandana tied over its back like a cape, running in ten different directions.

Banjo tugged on his leash.

I bent down beside Banjo so I could watch the dachshunds at ground level. They were taller than the grass but shorter than the flowers that three of them were trampling in the flowerbeds.

"Easy, boy," I said.

Banjo's eyes darted back and forth, watching all the puppies as they formed one small pack after another, ran away on their own, and kept playing keep away from the woman who was chasing them. Banjo moved his head only after a puppy started running toward the street. He looked at the puppy and then back at me.

The puppies only sped up as the woman became more panicked. Banjo's ears perked up and his body stiffened. One paw hovered in the air.

I put an arm around Banjo. His muscles were tight, but he didn't feel aggressive. More playful. And completely still, like a statue with a heartbeat.

Biscuit sat down and licked a paw.

The puppies were making bigger and bigger circles around the woman. One darted under a picnic table. Another was ransacking a flowerbed. A small tan blur skidded past us, ears flapping and cape flying.

It was hard to tell whether the children were cheering for her or the puppies.

"She's losing them," I said.

"She never had them," Erica said. Biscuit looked at the puppies, then at Banjo, and then put her head down between her feet.

"Need some help?" I called to the desperate woman.

"Yes! Please!"

I unclipped Banjo's leash.

Banjo bolted toward the black and tan puppy with the purple bandana that was headed for the street. It was the same motion he'd used with the deer. He cut a wide arc between the street and the pup and pushed him toward the other pups in the middle of the lawn.

The woman stood with one child in front of each leg, her hands resting on their shoulders. The boy reached her waist; the girl hit about mid-thigh and clung to her mother's leg like it was home base.

Banjo curved back around the pups, went wide to pick up a couple of renegades, then cut back to make sure no one escaped. One by one, he gently guided the puppies toward the center of the lawn, moving them with just enough eye contact to steer but never scare. No teeth. No lunging. Just graceful, four-legged problem-solving. Once the puppies were collected into a single squirming mass, Banjo sat panting beside them. The puppies stopped moving and looked admiringly at their new guardian protector.

"Almost got all of them," I said.

"Seven out of eight." Erica pointed to the carnations. "One is still digging over there."

The boy ran to fetch the puppy that was shoveling away in the flowerbed. The sister clung to her mother's leg.

"I don't know what just happened," the woman said. "I was watching them and then they just started running away." She looked at Banjo.

"He sure knew what to do," she said. "Is he a working dog?"

"He freelances," I said.

Banjo trotted back to my side like none of it had been a big deal. One ear flopped inside out.

I understood that Banjo was a foster dog, not a permanent pet. But I was realizing how much I was going to miss him if he was ever adopted. There was something pure about the way Banjo did things. He didn't think about it; didn't spend a lot of time rationalizing one way or the other. He just responded in the most natural way possible: Forcing other animals into compliance by acting like a wolf looking for lunch.

I didn't say it was romantic. I said it was pure.

Banjo was already eyeing the geese that were returning to the pond. I put him back on the leash.

"You've done enough for one day," I told him.

We walked on. Tai chi was happening in slow, mindful silence. The Regulars were in their usual spot, except for the man with the beard.

Erica stopped to admire the manzanita I'd planted.

That was when I saw the man from the table. Beard like a prophet. A blue windbreaker robe. Arms folded across his chest as he looked down at the manzanita.

He looked like someone who had just run into an old friend who happened to be a shrub.

I stopped alongside him. Erica stood on the other side of the manzanita.

"That wasn't here yesterday," I said, hoping to mask any involvement just in case he wasn't my secret accomplice.

The old man had a flat but satisfied smile. "No, it wasn't."

"Think it's some kind of message?" he asked without looking at me.

"Like a tiny living scroll," I said.

He must have noticed how Erica looked at me like I'd lost my mind. He stuck out his lower lip just a little and nodded his head.

"Like a scroll," he said. His smile grew as he looked at the manzanita that had no business being there. "I like that."

I pulled Banjo's leash and took a step back. I looked at Erica.

"I'd love to stay and look at this," I said, "but I have to finish this walk so I can get to work so I can come back at seven-thirty and walk Churchill."

"You're still walking Churchill?" She seemed surprised. "That's a long day."

"He's a long dog."

The old man looked at me more closely.

"Are you the guy who walks that basset hound?" he asked.

"That's me." I hadn't realized he was watching, but I guess I shouldn't have been surprised. Churchill was hard to miss and easy to keep up with.

"Not the most energetic creature, is he?" he asked.

I had to laugh. "He has his moments."

Erica and I were near the Corral before either of us said anything about what had happened or the man at the shrub.

"Are you going to tell me about what that was?" she finally asked.

"What?" I asked. "I saw someone admiring a tree and we talked about it."

"Give me a break," she said. "You did everything but tell the guy what you'd be wearing tonight."

I tried to laugh. "I did not."

She stopped.

"Look, I like you," she said. "I like the way you have with dogs. Dogs are great judges of character. And I like spending time with you."

"But…" I said.

Her eyes seemed bigger than before. "But I need to know what's going on. If he's a drug dealer, if you're setting up some kind of sketchy deal somewhere…"

She stopped.

"Actually," she said, "if he's any of those things, I don't want to know. But, I need to know if I need to find some other time to walk my dog. And maybe someone else to walk with."

"He's not anything like that," I told her. "He's one of the Regulars."

"The who?" she asked.

I pointed to the cluster of retirees sitting near the pond.

"The Regulars. Those old people who are always sitting over there."

"So that's how you know him?" Erica asked. "From just seeing him around the park when you were walking Biscuit?"

"That is the *only* way I know him," I told her. I reminded myself that as a Compliance Officer herself, Erica was a mandated reporter of such things.

"What was all that about having to come back here at seven-thirty?" she asked. "Why did you want him to know that?"

"I was thinking out loud about what I have to do today. It's just going to be too much," I said. "I think I'm going to have to drop Churchill."

She seemed to understand why I would drop Churchill. "I've been wondering how you were going to do that. But that still doesn't explain whatever that conversation with that man was about."

I stopped.

"I can't tell you what it was about," I said. "That's the honest truth. You're an Algorithmic Compliance Officer. I realize it's your job to make sure Halloween decorations are down by the second Monday in November—very important work, by the way—but you still work in Compliance."

"And what you're doing is an Algorithmic violation of some kind?" she asked.

"Sort of," I said. "But it shouldn't be."

It was time to see if Erica was a true believer in the Algorithms and their mandated reporter policies. I took a deep breath before I began.

"I was the one who planted the first flower for the flower trail," I told her. "Then someone—looks like it was that old men we met this morning, but I didn't know that at the time—planted a red flower. And then we just started going back and forth planting flowers.

"And that's it?" she said. "Two strangers planting flowers in the dark?"

"Today was the first time we've met," I said. "At least I think that was him that we met. It might be somebody completely different. I honestly don't know."

I told her about the scroll, about the letters, and about the violation notice.

"That's horrible," she said, which I saw as a good sign. "And you wanted him to know you'd read it?"

"Exactly," I said. "I wanted to know if he'd left the scroll. And I wanted him to know someone heard him. Or read him. Whatever. And that his secret was safe with me."

I paused when I realized what I'd done.

"But, now I'm telling you," I said. "A mandated reporter, no less. So much for that. I guess his secret wasn't that safe."

Erica smiled. "I promise not to tell. Do you know why he left something so personal like that for you to find?"

"That's why I told him I would be here tonight," I said. "I understand what happened to his granddaughter and how he feels responsible for that, even though he shouldn't. I just want to know why he wanted me to know about it."

I waited for it because I knew it was coming.

"But how did you know he'd stop at that…" Her face lit up as she stopped mid-sentence.

"You planted that tree!"

"I did. I'm your friendly neighborhood Guerilla Gardener.

"So you're going to meet him tonight?"

"I hope so."

Erica followed me to my car once we'd finished the lap.

"Same time tomorrow?" she said.

"Sure," I said. "If you don't mind being seen in the presence of a guerilla gardener who has people sending him secret messages in the park."

"I like gardeners," she said. "Guerilla or otherwise."

18

I thought about the old man that morning while I watered the petunias at Tuttle's. I still didn't know anything about him, other than he was somebody's grandfather and a fellow guerilla gardener.

I adjusted the drip line that kept the roots of the oak tree wet and wished I could install a drip line at the park for the manzanita.

When a customer asked if Hens and Chicks—*Sempervivum tectorum*—would trigger an Algorithmic Landscaping Compliance Violation, it took all I had not to say, "Who cares?"

"Yes, it would." I recited the statute and marveled at how quickly I could fall back into my old role.

My customer frowned but still admired the small pot and its smallish succulents.

"How many would you like today?" I asked.

She blushed. "I shouldn't really."

"No, you shouldn't," I said. "But you can." I smiled again. "And how many would you like today?"

She laughed.

I ran my finger along the sharp edge of one of the leaves.

"If it's any help," I offered, "in Roman times these were planted on rooftops to protect the home from lightning, fire, and tax collectors. *Sempervivum tectorum* literally means always on the roof."

The Algos used Latin names for plants to avoid sentimentality.

"No kidding," she said. "Well, you can never have enough protection from lightning and fire."

"Or tax collectors," I added quickly.

She put the flowerpot down and picked up the entire tray of one dozen plants.

I kept working but I was thinking about my after work appointment with the mystery man of Farrier Park. And my manzanita.

By the time I got home, Porter had moved everything out of the living room and the kitchen, broken or not. Banjo was herding the Roomba in the open space that had been our living room.

"I'm thinking I'll just start over," Porter said. "New everything. New couch. New table and chairs. Everything." He waved a finger in the air like a late night commercial for a discount furniture showroom.

"Everything, and I mean *everything*, must go!" he proclaimed.

"Let me know how much it costs and I'll pitch in," I told him. "I owe you that much."

"Don't worry about it," Porter said. "It's not like we're going to split it up when you move out."

I checked the time and headed for the door. I had a dog to walk.

And a grandfather to meet.

I picked up Churchill.

"I'm afraid I'm going to have to stop walking Churchill," I told Fred. "You were right. With my new job, it's just too much. I'm sorry."

"But he loves you!" Fred said. "You can see it all over his face."

"And I love him," I said, which may have been a stretch but it was close enough. "But I've got a new job and it's taking a lot of time."

"I understand." Fred kneeled down to Churchill's height, no small feat for a man of his age.

He scratched behind the basset's ears.

"Have a good walk, Churchill. Don't worry. I'll find someone else to take care of you." As if to underscore his message of needing help, Fred asked me if I could help him to his feet.

Over at the park, I saw the old man sitting alone again. He was at the same chess table. Same distance from the people I used to see laughing at his jokes.

I took a seat on the other bench. Churchill snorted and laid down beside me.

The old man extended his hand.

"Chris Schneider Nice to meet you."

"Wendell Jones," I said. "Nice to meet you." I was sure I'd never met him, but I recognized the name. That was never a good sign. I'd probably sent the guy a citation about illegal asparagus or something.

"Why'd you leave it?" I asked. I wasn't sure what to call him. It seemed wrong to call him by his first name. He felt like a "Mr. Schneider."

"Because I didn't know what else to do with it," he said.

He paused, I assume to collect his thoughts, and then continued.

"My granddaughter wrote something beautiful and true, and they called it a violation."

"I read the notice," I said, as if he wasn't the one who'd left it there for me to find. "It looks like the assignment was to use AI to write a reply to something." I tried not to sound like I supported the idea, but I had already fallen into the familiar routine of my former job of explaining violations.

"When she's older," I tried to explain, "she'll be required to use AI to write everything. They don't allow original writing in high school or college. Everything has to be written by AI."

"That's how it is now?" he asked.

His response was understandable. I wouldn't have known if Angela hadn't been a teacher.

"I'm afraid so," I said. "They've been doing that for several years now, ever since they started requiring government workers, journalists, and anybody else who does a lot of writing to use AI."

Mr. Schneider looked at the sky and then back at me.

"When did that start?"

"A few years ago. They start teaching them not to use their own writing around third grade," I said, remembering what Angela had told me. "By seventh grade, papers and assignments like your granddaughter's can have no more than 5% original content or it's an automatic F."

"Ironic, isn't it?" Mr. Schneider said. "Third grade was when they first told us our handwriting mattered. We practiced cursive for hours."

"I know," I said, "Now it's when they teach kids how to not write."

He wasn't looking at me anymore. Just the pond. The far side of the walking trail. The Regulars, still sitting at their usual tables, pretending they hadn't noticed me talking to him but not doing a very good job of it.

"It's funny how people act," he said. "The whispering started after she got that notification. Everyone suddenly knew what happened, or thought they knew. No one ever asked me. People I'd known for years started turning away when I'd come by."

He wasn't imagining it. Violations were published every week in the Peregrine Perch newsletter. Social death was the enforcement mechanism of choice on the Perch.

Mr. Schneider's frustration was palpable. "There were rumors that I had helped her cheat or had encouraged it somehow."

He stopped.

"I guess they're not rumors if they're true, huh?" he said. "I mean, she was responding to my letter."

I smiled sadly. It was the only thing I could think of to do.

"Then it grew," Mr. Schneider said. "These things always do. People saying things like 'Well, I heard....'."

"Nothing good ever follows that," I told him.

Mr. Schneider agreed.

"Exactly," he said. "And before you know it, kids are avoiding her. She's lost every friend she had. Nobody wants to be seen near me." He pointed to the Regulars.

"I used to sit over there," he explained. "I moved over here so they wouldn't have to."

"That's thoughtful of you," I said.

"You'd think so, wouldn't you?" He sighed. "They saw it as just another sign I'd done something wrong."

The sun was setting. The geese were getting ready for the night.

"I didn't want the only version of the story that survived to be the one they were telling," he said. He looked at the mountains along the horizon. "I wanted someone to know the truth, even if I didn't know them."

He looked at me and smiled.

"And then I saw your flower." His smile grew even wider. "Didn't know who planted it, but I thought—here's someone who might get it. Someone who won't twist it. Someone who'll just… read it and see it for what it is: A child thanking her grandfather for supporting her."

He was doing the same thing for his granddaughter that Angela had tried to do for her students. I wanted to tell her that I got it now. I understood. I just didn't know how to say that.

I was sure I shouldn't use AI to compose that message.

"Lies have a way of becoming the truth," Mr. Schneider said. "Once people hear it enough. Once enough people hear it. I wanted someone to know what actually happened, even if I didn't know who they were."

I sat quietly, remembering something I'd read a long time ago, before the Algorithms divided books into categories of "approved" and "unapproved". There's no telling how many Algorithmic Speech Compliance violations happened before people were required to use AI.

"A lie doesn't become truth just because it's accepted by a majority," I said.

Mr. Schneider glanced sideways at me then, the corners of his mouth twitching upward just slightly in recognition of the words.

"Booker T. Washington said that," he said. "A lie doesn't become truth, wrong doesn't become right, and evil doesn't become good just because it's accepted by a majority."

For a man who had brazenly ignored landscaping codes with no apparent fear, he looked rather sheepish.

"I'm kind of a history nerd."

I nodded. "Good quote."

"Great truth," he said.

He tapped the bench gently with one finger.

"But I didn't say what they were saying would become true," he said. "I said it would become *truth*. There's a difference. *True* is what actually happened. *Truth*—their truth, anyway—is the official version of the story, the version we collectively choose to accept. The version we are told to accept."

He looked back out across the park.

"Come with me," he said. "I want to show you something."

We walked to the manzanita. I smiled when I saw it again.

"Look closer." He pointed to the tree.

"What's missing?" he asked.

I didn't see anything new or notice anything missing.

"Nothing," I said. "Nothing's missing."

Mr. Schneider kneeled down beside the tree.

"This morning, there were at least a dozen berries on this thing, remember?" He waved his hand above the tree, as if expecting the few remaining berries to levitate towards him.

"This was covered in berries," he said.

"And now they're gone," I said. "How did I miss that?"

Schneider stood up and brushed off his knees.

"Carried away by birds, most likely," he said. Mr. Schneider panned the sky in search of potential seed carriers.

"That's how it starts." He turned to me.

I wondered if there would be a proliferation of manzanita shrubs around Peregrine Perch. Then I realized it wasn't my problem.

"Don't worry," he said. "I'm sure the birds will check with the Algos before they deposit any seeds."

We'd only gone a few steps from where the manzanita should have been before Mr. Schneider turned back to look at the empty space.

"I don't recall voting on what could and could not be planted in the park," he said.

"Democracies can't micromanage every decision," I reminded him.

"Maybe," Mr. Schneider said. "But the Algorithms don't seem to have any problem doing that. And it's not just flowers in the park. It's almost everything now."

"What are you saying?" I asked.

"I don't recall any discussion about any of this," he said in the same way a man might talk about how houses aren't supposed to burn down or it wasn't supposed to be this warm in June. "Forget the park. I don't recall any conversations about what I can plant in my own backyard."

I had to smile. "Are you saying you want public meetings with actual conversations and debate? The consent of the governed? All that?" I asked.

"Something like that, yeah." The older man gave a heavy sigh. "That was supposed to be the deal. These are not laws. There are no votes. No debate. The Algorithm doesn't care what you believe. It just runs."

"I think we all decided it was easier to just let the Algorithms do it," I said. "That's why we went this way."

"Right," he said. "It's government of the lazy, for the lazy, by the lazy."

19

I parked at my usual spot in the Farrier Parking lot the next morning. Banjo jumped out of the car and lunged for the track as soon as I attached the leash, but I pulled him back.

Instead, we went up Tall Grass Place, around Sagebrush Circle, and on to Orchard Trail.

My former street.

It wasn't the most affluent neighborhood on the Perch, but it was nice. Having Angela there made it nicer.

The house didn't feel like home after Angela left. In fact, it felt so little like home that I sold it a few months later and moved in with Porter.

I stood at the bottom of the hill that led into the neighborhood and thought about what it took to make that climb. It reminded me of how I felt looking up at El Capitan. I wondered if there was a mid-level, Sickle Ledge-style ledge where I could stop along the way. Maybe a neighbor's yard.

Then I realized that in the Perch, my old neighborhood was Sickle Ledge. A personal summit for those who were never meant to make it to the top.

I waved to one of my former neighbors who was working in their yard across the street, a man who once ate hamburgers cooked on my grill in my backyard.

When he didn't respond, I started crossing the street.

He turned to go inside.

"Joe!" I called. "Wait up."

Joe froze like a convict caught in the spotlight during a prison break.

He walked slowly over to me.

"You shouldn't be here," he said.

"Nice to see you, too."

"No, seriously," he said. "There was some mix up with the Algos. The people in your old house have been getting all of your compliance violations. Landscape violations, poop bag violations. All of it."

"I see the Algos are as efficient as always," I said.

"Where are you living now anyway?" he asked.

I wondered if Leonard had put a bounty on my head. Joe probably wouldn't collect it, but he might know someone who would. Word travels fast.

I bought the house before I met Angela. I'd managed to save enough money for the down payment and to qualify for a loan. I'd kept up with rising Algorithm fees, increased insurance rates, and property taxes that went up along with the value of the house, all without any increase in my pay. The house that was barely affordable when I bought it was becoming less so the longer I stayed.

I finally left because Angela was gone, but that simply moved up the timeline. We'd be facing the same choices if she'd stayed. I'd drawn the graph; the trajectory showed me falling off a cliff. I did not land in Peregrine Perch.

The new owners had a car parked in the driveway. I hoped for their sake that it was just someone visiting. If it wasn't, they were going to get a violation.

Their landscaping, however, was Algorithmic perfection.

I'd only been out of college about a year when I bought the house. It was right after I got my first real job that was even remotely related to my degree. I went into Compliance because "Algorithmic Landscape Compliance Officer" sounded more interesting than "insurance underwriter." Entry level pay was about the same. I didn't realize how quickly that would change over time, as my classmates' careers advanced and mine stayed the same.

And working for Leonard definitely lowered my quality of life, if not my standard of living.

Under Leonard and the constant revision of the Algorithms, my job became less about statistical analysis and more about writing up what essentially amounted to traffic tickets. Imagine Hercule Poirot as a Meter Maid. The job wasn't stressful in the traditional sense of the word, although no one likes the idea of telling a child they can't plant watermelons in their front yard. It was more like death by boredom. Murder by the mundane.

It was around that time that Porter came back into my life. We'd met in college. He was my brother from another mother. Our lives went in very different directions after we graduated. We even lost touch for a while. But when my life crashed, I called him to help me find the pieces. Or to give me a place to stay while I looked for them.

Porter's life hadn't worked out like he'd planned either. He was a communications major with aspirations of being a network anchorman. He'd told me about doing a live shot from an apartment fire when a fireman carrying a mother on one arm and two children with the other emerged from a burning building.

"The fireman was struggling," Porter had said, with his usual understatement.

Porter dropped the mic—while he was still on the air—and ran to help. He quit broadcasting and became a firefighter the next day.

He'd talked about fighting fires in Denver, around Elbert County, and in the mountains. He'd chased tornadoes across Colorado's eastern plains and on into Kansas and Oklahoma. He'd done avalanche rescues, lake rescues, and had retrieved more than his share of suburban cats from trees.

And then he quit.

He was still a certified EMT with the volunteer fire department in Elbert County. He carried an emergency radio alongside his fanny pack. But he didn't live at the firehouse. He didn't ride on the truck.

At some point, he'd bought the land in Elbert County—the land on which I now lived.

As Banjo and I walked back to the car, I realized I was thinking about Leonard and Porter so I wouldn't have to think about Angela. I'd come this way because I wanted to remember. When I got there, I realized I wasn't ready to remember everything.

Banjo pulled harder on the leash as we got closer to Farrier. We did one lap, talked to Ida and a few of the other Regulars, and then went back to Porter's.

I wondered, if Banjo was the foster dog that stayed, then was I the roommate who wouldn't leave?

20

Erica called the next morning to tell me she had an important meeting about the use of red, white, and blue crepe paper in Fourth of July decorations and would not be able to walk.

"I can walk Biscuit," I offered. It seemed like a nice thing to do.

It had rained the night before so the grass was still wet when Biscuit and I started around the path. The concrete was dry. Its hairless cat texture formed perfect rivulets for water to drain.

"This rain should be good for the manzanita," I told Biscuit. The grass was already responding to the moisture. It looked taller than it had the day before.

Biscuit and I arrived at the spot where the flower trail began, the site of the initial act of civil disobedience that started it all.

Our coneflowers were nowhere to be found.

I wondered if someone else had done the same thing I did and pulled the flowers without thinking. When it came to noncompliant vegetation, every citizen of Peregrine Perch was not only a mandated reporter, they were also encouraged to remove any infractions whenever possible.

And removing two coneflowers was certainly possible.

We walked on to the next stop along the trail. It was the same thing. Both flowers, my purple one and the red one left by Mr. Schneider, were gone. Same with the third stop. And the fourth.

I hesitated before walking on to the next stop, the manzanita.

The manzanita was gone.

I searched to see if someone had thrown the uprooted former-bonsai into the weeds, but there was no sign of it.

I thought about what might have happened to the manzanita as I checked on the oak at Tuttle's. I must have looked like I was in mourning when I went back inside. Tuttle ignored me at first. Then he asked what was wrong.

"I lost a tree this morning," I told him.

"The oak?" Tuttle raised one eyebrow and slowly nodded his head. "Don't write if off just yet. It's too early to tell."

"Not the oak," I told him. "Another tree. A manzanita shrub, actually."

"You're mourning a shrub?" he asked. "I like plants more than most guys, but we're talking some shrubbery. It's not like it was the last of the redwoods."

I explained about the coneflowers and the flower trail and how it lead up to my manzanita. I left out the part about the scroll. I didn't think I should share something that private.

"I've heard about this," Tuttle said. A broad smile formed on his wrinkled face. "You were the one behind that?"

I nodded to confirm. "I was. Well, me and this other guy."

Tuttle squinted one eye. "That other guy wouldn't happen to be Chris Schneider, would it?"

"How did you know that?" I asked.

Tuttle smiled. "Chris and I are old friends. He used to come in here every May looking for milkweed. Did that for years."

I flinched as I realized how I knew Mr. Schneider's name.

"I remember the milkweed," I said. "That was one of the first plants to be banned by the Algos. I wrote a lot of milkweed violations those first few years."

Tuttle looked disappointed but not surprised by my former life.

"You know Monarch butterflies only eat milkweed, right?" he said.

"I didn't at first, but Mr. Schneider made that quite clear in his response to the violation notice." I didn't usually read resident replies to violation notices, but Mr. Schneider's was handwritten in very human-sounding prose. I forwarded it to the Algorithmic Language Compliance Officers.

"But, it wasn't the butterflies," I said. "It was the caterpillars. People said they were squirming on their front porches. Thought they were worms. The Algos couldn't ban the Monarchs, so they banned the milkweed that brought them here."

"Because that made a difference?" Tuttle asked. "Chris started buying Milkweed every year after that happened. He bought more after the ban than before it, honestly. He was trying to replace what other people had removed. A few other people bought it too, but I always held some back for Chris."

Tuttle picked up his trash from lunch. "He hasn't bought any for a few years now. Must have gotten tired of paying the fines."

I wondered how many violations I'd written for Chris Schneider. I remembered at least three.

I wondered if he knew I was the one who signed them.

"So he's done this kind of thing before?" I asked.

"Not quite like this," Tuttle said. "He wasn't trying to make a milkweed trail or anything. He just liked having Monarchs around for his grandkids. And he understood that if you want butterflies, you have to accept the caterpillars."

Tuttle smirked. "I'm surprised your flower trail hasn't gotten a violation notice."

"Apparently it has," I told him. "They just sent them to the wrong address."

"Sounds about right," Tuttle said. "You know a manzanita won't survive out there for very long," he said. "You'll need to dig it up and bring it back inside at some point. But I'm sure it will enjoy its time outdoors before it dies."

"Doesn't matter," I said. "When I checked on it this morning, it was gone."

"Not a real surprise," he said.

"Along with all the flowers," I said. "Everything. The entire trail was pulled up by the roots. All they left was one of those compliance signs that they put in all the flowerbeds."

He swallowed hard and shook his head.

"That's too bad," he said. "And another reason to hate the Algos."

Banjo and I returned to the park that evening. The manzanita was still missing. Not a surprise, but still a disappointment.

I looked for Mr. Schneider, but he seemed to be missing, too.

21

Erica and Biscuit met us at the park the next morning for our usual morning walk. We paused and quietly noted each empty space where a pair of coneflowers had been. It was like finding an old diary only to discover that some of the pages were missing.

Neither of us said much. Then, without warmup or warning, Erica mentioned that she might lose her job. She said it like she was commenting on the weather or the death of a D-list celebrity.

"From Seasonal Compliance?" I asked. "You're talking about losing your job at Compliance? No offense, but what do you have to do to get fired from Seasonal Compliance?"

"Post on social media how much you hate your job," she said. "Not just the work. I loathe the concept of my job. The fact that it exists at all."

"And you put that online?" I asked.

"I did."

She didn't sound embarrassed.

"Were you sober?" It seemed like a reasonable question.

"I was," she said. "I was also mad at Leonard."

I had to laugh.

"What was the violation?" I asked. I could think of several possibilities just off the top of my head.

She explained it in the official language of a Compliance Officer. "Algorithmic Language Compliance: Section 291(b). 'The original content of your message exceeds the 5% maximum.'"

"So if you'd let AI write it, you'd be okay?"

"I would've been in compliance," she said. "Probably not okay. There would've been something else. At least a citation for unvetted sentiment."

She looked at me. "Any chance Tuttle needs help at the nursery?"

We were still talking about Erica's future job prospects when I spotted Mr. Schneider sitting alone in his new regular spot. Erica and I squeezed onto the opposite bench—two dogs, three humans, and a rising sense of unease.

"I got worried when I didn't see you yesterday," I told him. "Everything all right?"

"Everything's fine." He gave me a dismissive wave. "I was just rethinking things. Night before that, I had dinner plans—canceled. Same with poker last night. Five years running and suddenly no one can make it."

"Sounds like what Ida was saying happened to Mr. Johnson and the rosebush," I said. Mr. Schneider looked at me and nodded knowingly.

"And to my granddaughter," he added.

"And to me," Erica said. "And I only got a warning."

"It's my own fault," I said. "The manzanita was too big for them to ignore. Too easy to spot. They pulled it before it had a chance to take root. Then they took everything else while they were at it."

"They would've taken it anyway, just like they were going to pull up our flowers at some point," Mr. Schneider said. "I'm surprised it lasted this long."

Erica nodded. "They're behind. They haven't replaced Wendell. The Algos are still generating violation notices, but there's no one to verify them. No field inspections, no follow-ups."

Banjo whimpered. He was ready to move on.

"In a minute," I told him.

Mr. Schneider stared at the ornamental kale lining the walkway like it was an alien life form.

"We need to plant something bigger," I said.

"Your manzanita *was* bigger," Mr. Schneider said. "You saw what happened."

"Maybe in a flower bed?" Erica suggested.

"Too exposed," I said. "We need something that blends in long enough to stay but can still be seen by people who might be looking. Something people notice before Leonard does."

I scanned the park.

Then I saw it: the kale. Decorative. Uniform. Forgettable. Perfect.

"We've got zucchini plugs at the nursery," I said. "Mature ones. Already budding. Some already have tiny little baby zucchinis coming on. We could hide them in the kale."

Erica raised an eyebrow. "Zucchini?"

"They'll hide in the kale for a few days," I said. "Long enough to get established."

"Until there's giant zucchini all over the place," she laughed. "I can't give that stuff away fast enough in the summer."

"This isn't about the squash," I said. "Zucchini just happens to be convenient, prolific, and edible."

"Zucchini bread," Mr. Schneider said.

"Grilled with garlic and olive oil," I added. "Maybe a little smoked paprika." Living with Porter had taught me things.

Erica shook her head. "You're planning a squash insurrection."

Mr. Schneider shook his head and laughed. "As opposed to squashing an insurrection?"

Is there such a thing as a granddad joke?

"This is about standing up to the Algos," I said. "About telling the Perch we're done letting Algorithms run our lives. Curated media. Funneled truth. Lawn compliance. Take your pick. The vegetable isn't the point."

Mr. Schneider nodded. "The message is in the mulch."

"The more ridiculous, the better," I said. "Something that makes people look at it and say, 'You've got to be kidding me.'"

"Funny," Mr. Schneider said. "I often think 'you've got to be kidding me' when I hear about something new from the Algorithms."

Erica laughed again. "I can think of few things more ridiculous than Leonard having to explain to City Council why he's pushing a wheelbarrow full of zucchini out of the park."

"Exactly," I said. "The whole thing's a joke. Enforcement is just the punchline." I stopped because Mr. Schneider and Erica were both laughing so hard they wouldn't have heard me anyway.

"You laugh," I said once they'd stopped, "but if it sounds crazy to you, imagine how it'll sound when the Algos try to justify it."

Mr. Schneider still looked unsure.

"What made you think of zucchini?" he asked.

"I water them every day," I said. "These plants are ready to go. Some are already flowering. We'll have visible squash in less than a week."

"And you think zucchini can hide in the kale until then?" Erica asked.

"I think by the time anyone notices, it'll be too late," I told them. "We will have made our point."

I took inventory as I watered the zucchini later that morning. Fourteen plants, eight with buds, four with flowers, and one with a small zucchini just beginning to emerge. And one plant that didn't look so good. I asked Tuttle how long he wanted to keep them around.

"Somebody'll buy them," he said. "They're not costing us anything."

"Then I'm going to buy them all," I told him.

"Fourteen zucchini plants?" he asked. "Why?"

I wanted to tell him what we were doing. I already knew how he felt about the Algos. But we were on a "needs to know" basis. Ray Tuttle did not need to know. At least not yet.

"It's a gift for a friend," I explained.

"Does your friend run a soup kitchen?" he asked.

My zucchini plants and I got home from Tuttle's just as Porter was checking the mail.

It was Wednesday, the day the *Elbert County Tribune* came out. Once a full daily newspaper, it was now only a few pages delivered by mail once a week. But *The Trib* still covered the kind of local stories the internet ignored.

This week's front-page headline:

DOG HERDS DEER OUT OF HOME

Beneath it, an image from Porter's video of a deer in mid-air, leaping over the couch while Banjo nudged another toward the door.

"Banjo, an untrained Australian Shepherd, relied on his natural instincts to move the deer safely out of the house," Porter read aloud.

He glanced at me, eyebrow raised.

"Didn't they take out the couch right before we locked Banjo in your bedroom?"

"Yeah," I said. "But it sounds better than, 'They turned out the lights and opened the front door so the deer could see where to go.'"

"A little dramatic license never hurt anybody," Porter said. "At least you can tell this paper wasn't written by AI."

He blocked out words on an imaginary marquee.

"*The Trib:* Supporting human journalism since 1975."

The article closed with a note about adopting Banjo or other dogs from Pa's Dog Rescue, where he was one of many loving pets looking for a forever home.

"It won't be long now," Porter said. "Some rancher's going to see this and snatch Banjo right up. I just hope Pa screens these people before he sends them over here."

I met Erica and Mr. Schneider in the park several hours later, along with a groundskeeper named Jason who happened to be working the night shift when he saw us. Turned out he was the same groundskeeper that carefully trimmed around each of our flowers along the trail.

This time, he cut the lights.

Operation Zucchini began at 2300 hours.

Erica, Jason, and I took our spades and watering cans and carefully dug into the dirt between the kale plants. We placed the zucchini plugs about three feet apart. Altogether, they took up almost fifty feet.

"All we can do is wait," Jason said.

22

It was after midnight before I got home. A light was on in the shed. I figured Porter must have been working on something.

I went to bed but couldn't get to sleep. Erica, Mr. Schneider, and I had just committed multiple Algorithm violations, including trespassing, unauthorized planting, and destruction of public property, and probably something else along the way. I wondered whether those notifications would be sent to my former address like the others.

I also wondered how long it would take the Algos to update my personal information to reflect my current mailing address. So far, I'd avoided any forms that might give that away. Leonard cut off access to my supervisor email as soon as he got back from El Cap. As far as the Algos were concerned, I didn't have an email address.

I wondered what other mail I might be missing. Then I realized I didn't care.

The last piece of mail I'd gotten that mattered was the Valentine's Day card from Angela. She'd mailed it to me because she thought that would be more romantic. I'd said something about how I used to hang out at the mailbox around the holidays when I was a kid, waiting for Christmas cards or birthday cards or whatever the occasion might be that merited an actual letter. She'd remembered that.

Our mailbox sat on a post beside the driveway. I still checked it every day; more out of a sense of obligation than any sense of anticipation. Most of the time, it was ads and hard copies of bills I'd already paid online. I'd forgotten that holiday mail was even a thing.

I saw that envelope and felt loved. She'd designed and made the card herself, with a beautiful drawing of the two of us sitting in front of a heart-shaped sunset. Inside was a loving, handwritten message, the kind of message you send when your relationship isn't perfect but you're still trying. The kind of message that says, "I love you" even before you read those words above her signature.

And I gave her an Algorithm-approved Valentine's Day Card #58, selected online during my lunch break, printed on demand while I was at work. Then I picked up a dozen roses on the way home.

The timing could not have been worse. One of Angela's students had just told her how her mother was fined for planting an unauthorized living Christmas tree too close to the sidewalk. The family was also fined for having Christmas lights up past the January 10 removal date, but that was from another department and had nothing to do with me.

Angela did not appreciate that detail.

She didn't leave because of the card. She left because the card was the last in a long string of arguments and frustrations, most of which could be traced to my commitment to the Algorithms I enforced.

People in Compliance tend to follow the rules.

Until they don't.

I wasn't following the rules when I tossed out the violation notice about Angela's goldenrod outside her classroom window. And going out with someone—Angela—while they were under an active Landscape Compliance investigation was definitely against the rules. I was pretty sure that even asking her if she'd like to go to dinner a week later was probably a violation. Completely losing all records of the goldenrod planted beneath her classroom window and then asking her if she'd move in with me a month later was almost certainly a violation.

The best relationship of my life happened when I ignored the rules. I should have learned something from that. Instead, I started pointing out infractions in our neighbors' yards when Angela and I walked through the neighborhood.

Teachers tend to be naturally nurturing people. Angela, it seemed, was even more so than most.

There is nothing nurturing about Algorithmic Landscape Compliance.

It's the opposite of nurturing.

23

For the next two weeks, Erica, Mr. Schneider, and I brought watering cans at night when there wasn't enough rain, kept the zucchini vines tucked amongst the kale where they couldn't be seen, and watched the Regulars pretend they hadn't noticed the bright orange flowers poking out among the kale or the man sitting alone at the chess table less than a hundred feet away.

"I've never seen kale bloom like that," I overheard one of the Regulars saying.

"That's not kale blooming," Ida replied. "It's something else. Looks like some kind of squash. Maybe a pumpkin."

"Those are daylilies," said the former county official. "I got a code violation for those last year. Said they were of inconsistent size and shape."

"If that's the case," Ida replied, "we're all in trouble." All the Regulars laughed. It had been a while since that happened.

Mr. Schneider's exile left the group floating with no sun to orbit. There was no storytelling. No jokes, or thoughts about the news of the day, or stories about grandchildren. Without Mr. Schneider to drive the discussion, there was no one to restart the conversation once the small talk inevitably stalled.

Instead of a circle, they'd broken into loose clusters. Two older women shared a table, but only because it was a convenient place to set their coffee. A few men sat nearby in silence. Three others remained at the old circle's center, like guests at a party where the chairs had been taken to another table. It really didn't seem to matter where they were sitting. No one was talking very much.

Mr. Schneider's eyebrows lifted slightly when someone walked in his direction. The faint crease of hope that appeared across his forehead disappeared just as quickly when they nodded politely and kept on walking or stopped to speak to someone else along the way. It was the look of someone wishing someone would talk to him while praying that no one would notice he was there.

They all looked like they were waiting for someone to start their day. It was as if they knew each other, but still needed permission to connect.

Mr. Schneider was more present in his absence than he had been when he was telling stories a few days before.

I wondered if I'd feel that way about Banjo when Pa found a permanent home for him.

Pa dropped by our house to check on Banjo the morning after the *Tribune's* story came out. I was about to take Banjo for his walk when his phone rang.

"Lloyd Hainer just lost an Australian Shepherd," Pa said. "He's looking for a puppy." He looked at the ID and signaled for me to wait.

"This is him," Pa said. "I need to take this."

Porter and I nodded. "Sure."

"Hi Lloyd," Pa said when he answered the phone. "I'm going to put you on speaker so Michael Porter can hear you. He' been fostering the dog. You can ask him about Banjo."

"That Porter's an interesting fellow, isn't he?" Lloyd must not have known he was already on speaker. "But, he knows dogs. I'll give him that."

"Well, thank you," Porter said.

The voice on the phone hesitated for just a moment before he finished his greeting.

"Oh, hi," he said. "Sorry. Didn't know you were going to hear that."

"I've been called a lot worse than interesting," Porter said.

"You understand he's not trained, right?" Pa explained to Lloyd when he came over to pick up Banjo. "Great dog. Incredible instincts. But he does not know commands and he's never been around sheep or cattle. At least not as far as I know."

"Just deer," Porter added.

"I know," Lloyd said. "We'll have to work with him. But you say he's got good instincts?"

"Most natural herder I've ever seen," Porter said. I nodded my head, remembering how Banjo rounded up those puppies at the park.

"Doesn't know anything," Porter continued. "You can say 'that'll do' all day long and he won't turn around. Means nothing to him."

"But you think he can learn?" Lloyd asked.

Pa and Porter looked at each other, weighing what they were going to say next.

"I don't see why not," Pa said. "He's only six months old, so the age is right. He's got the tools. He just needs someone to show him how to use them."

Lloyd and Pa were back in our still empty living room three days later. Banjo was the only one who looked like he was glad to be there.

"Not working out?" Pa asked.

"Afraid not." Lloyd looked at Banjo. "Real shame, too. You're right about the instincts. Amazing. Like watching ballet."

I couldn't help but to look at Lloyd. He did not impress me as a ballet fan.

"My daughter dances," he said, as if he was accustomed to explaining himself.

He gently patted the dog he had hoped to train.

"He started out great," Lloyd said. "But then his circles kept getting tighter. His nudges became nips. And then he jumped and bit a ewe on the flank."

"That's no good," Porter said. "Are the sheep okay?"

"I managed to get them calmed down before they trampled each other to death." He looked as if he was addressing Banjo directly. "Broke skin when he bit that ewe. No stitches or anything, but still. It's not good."

Pa didn't want to have to rehouse this dog.

"You don't think you could train that out of him?"

"Probably, but not in the amount of time I have." Lloyd handed the leash to Pa. "Jill always trained the dogs. And she can't do that anymore."

"How is Jill?" Porter seemed genuinely concerned.

"Better," Lloyd said. "I was helping her out of the bathtub and dropped her. We decided she should live in that place over by the Post Office after that. I hate that, but I don't want to drop her again. She doesn't need a broken hip on top of everything else."

He looked at Porter and tried to smile.

"She misses her gardening." Lloyd cleared his throat and blinked a couple of times.

"But about your dog," he said after a long quiet moment. "Remember that baseball player that pitched for the high school a few years ago? Great arm. One of the fastest fastballs I've ever coached. But he also set the league record for the number of batters he hit. He'd be two outs into an inning and then walk three in a row."

Porter nodded his head but said nothing.

Lloyd looked at Banjo. "Same problem here. Incredible talent. Great instincts. But he's going to end up hurting my sheep."

"Think he'd be better with cows?" I asked.

Lloyd shook his head. "He'd end up getting kicked in the head or run over in a stampede."

"Well," Porter said, "we don't want that."

And Banjo was back with us again, just in time for me to go to work.

Tuttle hadn't asked me to, but I'd been checking on the oak he'd dropped off that day behind the loading dock. It reminded me of the manzanita on the ledge. Both of them trying to survive in a place they weren't meant to be.

The manzanita on El Capitan made it. I wasn't so sure about the oak in the parking lot.

I wasn't doing much for it, just checking to make sure the root ball wasn't soggy and shooing away the rabbits that kept eating its leaves. I saw a cat and her six newborn kittens nestled in the thinner upper branches of the tree on a bed of oak leaves.

"You can stay there for now," I told the cat. "Try to do something about these rabbits."

The door to Porter's work shed was open when I got home from Tuttle's that evening. Either Porter was out there or he'd left it open while he ran inside. I'd never been in there, but I went over to just to check.

The shed smelled like sawdust and paint. The broken kitchen table leaned against the back wall, its legs in a neat pile beside it, as if it had died peacefully after arranging its own limbs. Porter stood in front of it like someone paying their respects.

While Banjo watched, Porter picked up a small brush and began clearing the grooves where the deer's hooves had splintered the table's edge. He paused to blow the dust off, watched it swirl in the light.

A glance at the pegboard with its outlines of tools told me what tools Porter planned on using: a pull saw, a mallet, a file. Every tool had an outline, just like every day had its clipboard.

Everything else in the shed was covered in tarps to protect it from sawdust and sunlight.

Some things were obvious. The shape of a lawnmower. A welding setup, with sheet-covered tanks that could easily be mistaken for ghosts when the only light in the shed was the moonlight coming through the door.

Wooden legs that were probably holding up a dresser peeked out from beneath one blue tarp. The scrolled base of a hat stand or an umbrella holder or something poked out from beneath a heavy gray canvas. Some were covered in a thick layer of dust. Others had less dust and more handprints, as if they had been worked on or at least touched more recently.

Knowing Porter, I assumed the folded tarps in the corner represented projects of the past.

The craftsman circled the top of our former table like he was sizing up an opponent.

"I thought you were going for something newer," I said.

"I got tired of looking for a new table," Porter said. "Figured I'd just rebuild this one." He rapped his knuckles on the table top. "Good wood."

"Yes." I ran a finger along the table's broken top. "You can tell that by the way it split and then collapsed when the deer landed on top of it. The legs were especially impressive that way."

"Yeah," Porter said. "Good wood."

24

"Jason told me about your project at the park," Tuttle said while I watched him adjust the oak's drip line the next morning. "Said he was glad he could help."

"Jason?" I asked. "I don't know any Jason."

"He's the gardener at Farrier," Tuttle said. He stood up and wiped his hands. "For all of the Perch, actually. Friend of mine. He orders all their landscaping stuff from me. He came by yesterday after you left."

That made sense. You could feed a small country with fourteen zucchini plants and still have enough left over to make zucchini bread for a large family. Tuttle probably suspected something was up when he saw me leave with fourteen zucchini plants yesterday. Makes sense that he would tell his friend, especially if this Jason was on our side. That explains why he was there.

I hoped.

"But you hate the Algos," I said.

"I do," Tuttle said, "but Jason isn't an Algo. He's just a guy who loves plants and is trying to make Farrier Park as nice as possible, even though he's stuck with these ridiculous Algorithms and their idiot enforcers telling him what to do."

"As a former idiot Algorithm enforcer," I began, "why do you hate the Algos? I mean, I have my reasons. Everybody has their reasons. What's yours?"

"You mean other than the fact that I had to relocate to the edge of town?" he asked.

Tuttle took a deep, calming breath.

"I hate the whole idea of it," he said. "More specifically, I hate that they are always trying to force me to stop selling plants that aren't on their approved list. They seem to forget that I'm pulling in customers from all around here, not just Peregrine Perch. I have people who drive up all the way from Colorado Springs. And probably other places, too."

"So they want to force their protocols on everyone?" I said. "That's what you hate?"

"Yes," he said. "Look, if those people on the Perch want to live that way, more power to them. But when they start telling me that I can't sell milkweed to someone in Elbert county because they've banned it on the Perch, that's wrong. Or I can't sell Brandywine tomatoes—the best tomato around, if you ask me—because their leaves and tomatoes don't comply to 'Algorithmic size conformity protocols.'"

He stopped talking for a moment, but picked up again with even more anger.

"They actually threatened to pull my contracts with the city over that Brandywine thing," Tuttle said. "I still sell them, but customers have to ask for them by name. I keep them in a backroom in the greenhouse."

"They must be secret," I said. "I don't think I've ever seen them."

"You have to earn that," he said. He walked me back to the secret tomato sanctum. "The whole thing is ridiculous. It's like me saying, 'I don't like curly fries, so you can't have any.'"

I understood, although I never liked curly fries, either.

Officially, the reason for the "voluntary restrictions" on selling banned plants to customers who live in other counties was to prevent those plants from voluntarily popping up in Peregrine Perch. Seeds know how to get around. They travel on the wind, or they get carried off and dropped by birds. Or they travel on people's clothing; or on animals. A complete quarantine would be impossible without the surrounding counties doing the same.

Even if those counties didn't want to cooperate.

"That's fine if they want to live that way," Tuttle said. "I don't, which is why I don't live on the Perch. It's why my store is no longer on Main Street. I'm not going to force their rules on my customers."

I was standing by the oak later that day when one of the landscaping contractors walked up and asked about buying the tree. Tuttle recognized him and followed him over.

"It's yours for two thousand," Tuttle told him.

"How much will it go for if it doesn't sell and you have to chop it into firewood?" the contractor asked.

"We're a long way from firewood." Tuttle laid his hand on the tree trunk. "It'll sell."

"But suppose it doesn't." The contractor pulled a leaf from the top of the tree. "What do you think? Two, maybe three hundred dollars worth of firewood in there?"

"I suppose." Tuttle shrugged. "But that's not going to happen."

"So," the contractor began. "If I wait a few weeks, I could buy the tree for $300 and save you the trouble of having to cut it up."

"It doesn't work that way." Tuttle smiled. "And, in your case, it's never going to work that way. I'll burn this tree and toast marshmallows on the flames before I sell it to you for three hundred dollars. And I will enjoy every bite."

Tuttle gave the drip line another unnecessary check as a signal to the contractor that it was time for him to leave.

"He's not getting this tree," he told me after the contractor left. "But, he's right. It's dying faster than I thought it would. It may be time to cut our losses, so to speak, and chop up the oak."

"Mind if I work with it?" I asked. After losing the manzanita, I needed something to care for.

The older man looked at me.

"I really don't think this tree is going to make it," Tuttle said. He looked at the tree and then back at me. "It's not in the way here. See what you can do with it. But I'd be sharpening that ax if I was you."

Time was working against all of us. I was preparing to lose Banjo. I didn't want to lose the tree.

Three days and the creation of "Easter Egg: Zucchini Edition" had begun before Banjo got another chance for a permanent home.

The zucchini harvest began when Mr. Schneider rose from his seat at the chess table, took out his pocketknife—he was of a generation of men that always had a pocketknife with them—and casually walked past the Regulars. He stopped to kneel down beside the kale, rummaged around in the leaves, and pulled out a zucchini large enough that the Regulars at the table could see it.

"How'd they react?" I asked him when he told me.

"It took them a while to realize what it was. A couple of them pointed at me while I was walking. I think they thought it was a stick or something." He laughed softly. "They became more interested when I sliced off a piece and started eating it. They started creeping forward in fits and starts, like they'd just been let out of a locked room and weren't sure what they were allowed to touch."

"Like those chimpanzee rescue videos when they see grass for the first time?" I asked.

Mr. Schneider smiled, nodded, and pointed a finger at me.

"Yes!" he said. "I was trying to think what that reminded me of. Anyway, Ida must have figured out that I was involved somehow. She walked over to the chess table and thanked me. One of them went home and came back with a big thing of Ranch dressing. Even offered some to me."

Any zucchini trepidation that might have remained passed by the time I saw the Regulars the next morning. Banjo, Biscuit, Erica, and I watched several senior citizens stride boldly forth, kitchen knives in hand, to harvest the bounty of fourteen prolific zucchini plants. You would have thought a great famine had come to an end and soon they would be breaking zucchini bread together.

I looked at Banjo and wondered how much time I had left with him. I didn't have to wonder long. Another potential owner was talking to Porter when Banjo and I got home.

The man crouched down to Banjo's level and held out his hand. Banjo sniffed it, looked at me, and sat down.

"Come on, boy," the man said.

Banjo slowly lowered himself to the ground like someone was letting the air out of him. Legs folded, chest flat, chin down. He wasn't aggressive. He just wasn't going to move.

Banjo stayed still while this stranger attached the leash to his collar, but when the man gave a gentle tug, Banjo went limp. A hundred percent deadweight. He looked like a furry black and white pancake on the ground.

The man bent down and scooped Banjo into his arms. Banjo stayed limp for about two seconds. Then a twist. A back leg pushed against the stranger's chest. A front paw grabbed for air and hit the man on the nose. One last final twist and his captor dropped him. Banjo landed hard but came trotting straight back to me like nothing happened.

He sat between Porter and me.

The man sighed. "Well, I guess he's made up his mind."

"Looks that way," Porter lifted Banjo to his chest with no problem.

"Looks like you'll be staying with us."

25

Expectations grew along with the zucchini vines. One woman with a couple of kids asked Mr. Schneider if he knew if the park would be planting any other vegetables later that summer.

"I don't know anything about any of this," Mr. Schneider said. Then he winked at her and walked away.

As more people learned about the zucchini, Ida and some of the others began to worry that someone might harm the plants.

"You mean someone other than Leonard?" I asked.

"Well, him too," Ida said. She nodded toward the skateboarders. "But it could be anyone. You never know with people these days."

Ida gripped my arm and slowly lowered herself beside the kale and zucchini.

"Look," she said. "Someone pulled up an entire plant, roots and all."

"They were probably just trying to get a zucchini," I told her. I tried not to react, but the uprooted zucchini plant, exposed and vulnerable with no natural defenses of its own, was a disturbing sight.

Ida put the roots back in the ground and pushed dirt around it. It wasn't a great job of plant recovery, but I didn't want to criticize her effort. We were in big trouble if we were depending on Ida to protect the zucchini.

I helped her back up.

"I think we'll be okay," I told her. But she did have a point. As word spread and more people knew about our zucchini in the park, it seemed inevitable that someone would come for the plants.

Porter was working in the shed again when I got home. He jumped when I opened the creaking door, then immediately grabbed a tarp and threw it over what he was working on. I couldn't tell anything about it other than it was an odd height.

"What's up?" he said.

"Some of the Regulars are worried that someone is going to attack the zucchini when they're not there," I told him.

Porter put his tools back on the pegboard and met me at the door.

"How would someone do that when the Regulars are there all the time?" Porter asked. "That's why they're the *Regulars*."

"They meant at night," I said. "One of the men volunteered to spend the night in the park, but he couldn't figure out where to plug in his CPAP machine."

"Yeah," Porter said. "The last thing you want is for them to find some dead old guy in your vegetables."

That was an image I had not considered.

"Right," I said. "So, want camp out with me?"

Porter shook his head.

"Negative," he said. "I haven't been to Farrier Park in years, not since they fined me for excessive dog walking."

"Excessive dog walking? How many dogs did you have on your leash?"

He held up five fingers in case I needed a visual aid. "Two Chihuahuas and three teacup poodles, so five altogether. But they were all small dogs. Nobody over six inches tall. They popped me for a hundred dollars. If I'd known they were going to do that, I would have brought six Rottweilers. Would have been more entertaining."

"No dogs this time," I said. "Not even Banjo. Just you, me, and the zucchini."

Porter looked at the tarp-covered project behind him and the stack of cut boards sticking out from another tarp on the floor.

"I've got all this to do," he said. He looked around. "OK. I'm in. When do I report for duty?"

The park closed at ten o'clock, but there was no fence or gate to lock shut.

We arrived around eleven.

"We used to put up a tent and camp over here when I was a kid," Porter said. "Before Peregrine Perch was even a thing. This was all just open land."

"Did you circle the wagons at night and keep the womenfolk inside?" I asked.

"As a matter of fact, we did." Porter winked. "Love on the Perch, baby."

"Well, we don't have tents or covered wagons," I told him. "We'll just have to circle the lawn chairs."

We set up our chairs. Porter opened a thermos of coffee and offered me a cup. I checked my phone. Porter read a book.

Neither of us said it, but after an hour, it was clear no one was coming. No skateboarders. No vandals. No militant vegetarians coming to rescue the squash. The only excitement came from a raccoon running out from under the kale with a zucchini.

"I think we found your thief," Porter said.

He flipped a page, didn't look up.

"You didn't come out here because of the zucchini, did you?" he asked.

I thought before I answered.

"I don't know," I said. "Maybe a little."

He nodded like that tracked.

"Who asked you to watch the place?"

"Her name's Ida," I said. "She's one of the Regulars."

Porter closed the book, used his thumb as a bookmark.

"So you're here because she was worried," he said. "That makes sense."

I didn't say anything.

Porter stretched his legs out, ankles crossed.

"I've seen guys run into burning buildings for people they didn't know," he said. "Happens all the time. At least you know… Imma? Edna?"

"Ida," I reminded him. "She's been checking the zucchini like it's in the ICU."

We heard the sprinklers turn on in the middle of the lawn.

"We're gonna get wet," I said.

"We might."

"So, I'm here for Ida," I said. "Why are you here?"

Porter looked at me. "Because you asked me."

He looked to the east, away from Denver, to where the light from the city didn't obliterate the stars in the night sky.

"In 2002," he said, "we got called out to the San Juans. There was a wildfire west of Vallecito, way up in the mountains there. It looked like it was going to go fast. They wanted us there in case it did."

"You're talking about firefighters?" I asked.

"No, the Boy Scouts," he said. "Yes, I am talking about firefighters."

He swatted me with his book and looked back at the sky.

"We hiked for two days with full gear," Porter said. "Twenty-pound packs, hand tools, just enough food to get us through three shifts. But when we got there, it started raining. Not forecast rain. It was just mountain weather doing what it does. The fire was mostly out. Still smoking in spots, but no real threat left."

"You sound disappointed," I said.

"It was a long hike," he said. "We spent two more days walking the perimeter, eating protein bars, and digging around in the mud just making sure. Some of the locals started bringing us dinner."

I looked out at the zucchini plants. Quiet. Undisturbed.

"And this feels like that?" I asked.

"Not at all," he said. "But I like telling that story." He stood up to stretch. "But, now that you mention it, waiting in the dark for nothing to happen is what hope looks like sometimes."

26

Things settled into a routine after that. I started doing one last check on the zucchini right before the park closed. Sometimes Ida would join me. She told me that she lived across the street. I'd walk her home when she decided to leave.

Everything was going well until one morning when Erica and I saw Leonard talking to the Regulars. They seemed to be arguing. We moved in close enough to hear but not close enough, we hoped, to be noticed.

Leonard was writing tickets for "vandalism of city property."

"Mr. Schneider, this is your fourth violation." Leonard smiled as he handed him the ticket. "Congratulations. You're in the bonus round."

"His fourth violation?" I stepped up to defend him as best I could. "How did you get four violations out of this?"

"He's talking about something else," Mr. Schneider said. "And the last one was over three years ago."

"Doesn't matter," Leonard said. Then he looked at me. "Algos are like elephants. They never forget."

I was glad Leonard didn't elaborate about Mr. Schneider's previous violations.

"But how is this vandalism?" I demanded.

"Those plants belong to the city," Leonard lied. "When you cut that stem, you vandalized city property."

"That's ridiculous," Mr. Schneider told him. "The city had nothing to do with this."

"Then tell me who did," Leonard said. "I'll write them up for an unauthorized landscaping violation and tear up everyone else's ticket."

Leonard looked at the Regulars. One by one, the seniors citizens shook their heads. That's how revolutions work sometimes. Slowly, and with arthritis.

"The zucchini just showed up," Schneider said. "I hear they do that sometimes. Apparently volunteering is a big thing in zucchini culture."

"Enjoy it today," Leonard sneered. "By tomorrow, it's gone. I've been wanting to get rid of that kale mess for a while."

Leonard turned to me.

"I'm not going to lie," he told me. "We need you back. We're drowning in unfiled violations. There's no one to go out and inspect on site, which is how messes like this zucchini thing get started."

"I like zucchini," I said.

Erica agreed. "I'm good with zucchini." Mr. Schneider nodded in agreement.

Leonard, per usual, ignored the comments of others.

"You can be Director of Landscape Compliance," he told me. "I'll make you a new badge and give you a bigger cubicle."

"After all we've been through," I said. "Not even a vest? That makes me sad, Leonard."

"It pays more," he countered.

"I like dogs," I said. "Dogs and zucchini. That's pretty much my life these days."

"We're going to have to do some reshuffling." He faced Erica. "If Wendell doesn't come back, your job might not exist."

"Are you firing me?" she asked.

"That's up to Wendell," he said.

Classic Leonard. Outsource the cruelty.

"Let me know by tomorrow," he said in his best manager voice.

"Or what?" I asked. "You'll shoot the zucchini?"

"I'm already doing that." He looked at Erica. "Along with your forget-me-nots."

"What?" Erica's face turned white.

"Your forget-me-nots," Leonard repeated. "Wendell wrote up the violation about a week before he quit. I found it when I was going through the backlog of stuff he didn't get finished."

"I planted forget-me-nots because they were my mother's favorite," Erica explained. She sounded almost as if she was apologizing. Her tone turned angry when she looked at me.

"Those are native plants," she said. "I looked it up."

"You should have looked up the Code instead," Leonard sneered. "Wendell, you want to tell her why you issued that violation?"

I closed my eye, took a deep breath, and recited the code.

"Forget-me-nots present a threat to containment protocols. They are considered prolific and aggressive and have been known to spread into pathways and neighboring properties."

"Wow," was all Erica managed to say.

"There you have it," Leonard said. "From the man who wrote the violation."

I seethed.

"There was a reason that was still on my computer and not in a hard copy for delivery," I said. "I went out and looked at it. She had a small patch behind her garage surrounded by gravel. They weren't going to spread. And, even if they had, they're a native species."

That answer wasn't good enough for Erica.

"Then why did you write it up at all?" she asked.

I glared at Leonard for putting me in this position.

"Documentation," I said. "In case there was a future infraction."

Leonard smiled. "I rest my case. Wendell, let me know what you decide. I'll decide what to do with your documentation."

We watched him slither away.

"I am so sorry," I said once he was gone.

"You can't go back," Erica said. "I mean, who would write up people's favorite flowers if you did."

"I'm sorry," I said. "But now, I almost have to. I could use the money and you don't need the hassle."

"You don't have to," she said. "I'll plant more forget-me-nots next year."

Erica said the vet who gave her Porter's number when she was looking for someone to walk Biscuit was looking for a tech. Just someone to help around the clinic. She'd call him. It'd be a pay cut, but she didn't want to work for the Algos anymore.

"Tired of the Algos, or tired of Leonard?" I asked.

"There's a difference?" she said.

"Not really."

Banjo ran straight for Porter's work shed when we got home, a low-flying missile of black and white fur. I was glad the door was open, so she didn't blast through it.

"Banjo!" I heard Porter yell from fifty feet away. "You're home! Come to papa!"

Porter had restored two of the table's legs using a peg and notch system he'd devised to hold the broken pieces together.

"It's going to be about an inch lower than it was, but it'll still be comfortable. And sturdy." He inspected one of his reconfigured legs. "Going for more of a Japanese aesthetic. Wabi-sabi, baby! Wabi-sabi!"

I pondered the beautiful imperfections of my own life the next morning as I checked on the oak. The leaves were beginning to look more grayish than green. Some had already started turning brown. And the smell of constantly wet burlap around the root ball was becoming too strong to ignore.

"I heard Leonard's going to take out your zucchini," Tuttle said while he watched. "That's a shame. I tried to get them to line that walkway with fruit trees. I thought that'd be a nice touch, a nice thing for the community. They went with the kale instead."

"Kind of sums up the entire Algorithmic mindset, doesn't it?" I put my hand on the root ball to see if it was dry. "Why do something useful when you can do something that looks busy and accomplishes nothing?"

Tuttle ignored my dig at the Algos.

"What are you going to do if he takes them out?" Tuttle wanted to know. "How do you top something like fifty feet of zucchini vines?"

"We're just going to have to plant something bigger."

27

I was contemplating what might be bigger than fifty-plus feet of interwoven zucchini vines when a car I did not recognize pulled into the parking lot.

"I need some tomatoes!" The woman's voice sounded happy, excited, and a little conspiratorial.

I knew the voice immediately.

It was Angela.

"I've got some cherry tomatoes over here," Tuttle told her. "And some Big Boys and some Cherokee Purples back there too."

"That's not what I came here for," Angela said. I could see her eyes narrow from my hiding place behind the hanging plants. "I know what you've got back there. I want the Brandywines."

"What makes you think I have Brandywines?" Tuttle sized her up as he spoke, looking for signs that she might work for Leonard. "Brandywines aren't allowed on Peregrine Perch. The Algorithms banned those years ago."

"I know," she said. "And I know you have some. I'd like some, please."

"Are you with Compliance?" he asked. As if Compliance Officers were required to identify themselves.

"No," Angela said. "I can't even afford to live on the Perch anymore."

I'd been doing my best to disappear ever since Angela stepped out of her car, but hearing that her life had been just as disrupted as mine was more than my curiosity could stand.

I turned to face the music. And my ex.

"I can help her," I offered.

Angela slowly turned toward me.

"Wendell?" she asked. "What are you doing here?"

"I work here," I told her.

"You work here?" She sounded like I'd said I was living under a bridge, which would have been better than if I'd told her I was living with Porter.

"Yes." I cleared my throat. "I am the Vice President in charge of Arboreal Health. Would you like some goldenrods?"

"Only if I can rub your nose in them."

Tuttle rolled his eyes and walked away. "Show her what she wants," he said.

Angela walked with me to the inner sanctum. We passed by Tuttle's rosemary along the way. I pinched off some leaves without even thinking about it. I dropped them to the floor so Angela wouldn't see me sniffing them.

"You left Compliance?" she asked.

"I did."

"Tired of watching kids get tagged for original thought?"

"Tired of pretending I wasn't."

That got a blink out of her. Progress.

"I heard about the zucchini." She showed a begrudging smile of approval. "They're calling it an 'unauthorized propagation event.'"

I picked up a tray of Brandywines and handed the entire thing to her.

"That's a lot of tomatoes," she said. "I'm going to put some of these back."

"Leonard offered me a promotion if I came back," I told her while she put about half the plants back on the shelf.

"Did you laugh in his face?" she asked.

"I'm considering taking the job," I said. "It's complicated."

"I'm surprised to hear you say it's complicated," she said. "You usually stay in the lines and make sure everyone else does the same."

I offered to carry the tray for her but she said she could do it. She put what was left in the tray of forbidden tomatoes on the counter.

"I got fined for not turning in a kid who wrote a sonnet about his dead hamster," she said. "I mean, technically it was a gerbil, but the grief was real. So was the writing."

She looked at me to let that sink in.

"Unlike what I can say about anything I got from you," she said, just in case I'd missed the point.

"Will there be anything else?" I asked just before I rang her up. At least I no longer had to think of anything to say. All that was left was, "Thank you and enjoy your plants."

I handed her credit card back to her.

That should have been the end of it.

"I'm sorry about what happened," I said. "For all of it. For not supporting you, for not understanding, for all of it."

"And the card?"

"I should have written the card myself." I should have stopped there, but I didn't."

I should have stopped there.

"But, in my defense," I added, "I did edit it. The 'I love you' was mine."

Her eyebrows went up at the same time her head tilted and her mouth opened. It was a very loud silent scream.

"Really?" she said through perhaps the fakest smile to never appear in a toothpaste commercial. "Well, that's just sweet, Wendell. Thank you so much for that original thought."

I wanted to ask how she was doing. I wanted to ask if we could get together some time.

I settled for asking if I could carry the tomato plants to her car.

"I've already told you I've got these," she said. Her expression softened just a little. I'm not sure that someone who didn't know her would have noticed the difference. But I did.

"But thank you," she said. "And I hope things work out for you."

"You too." I stepped toward her. Without thinking, I opened my arms for a hug.

"What are you doing?" she said. "We had a civil conversation. That does not entitle you to a hug." She pointed to the oak.

"Hug the tree," she told me. "It'll mean more to both of you."

Tuttle stepped up beside me.

"Friend of yours?" he said.

"No," I told him. "Just someone I know."

"I like her spirit," Tuttle said.

Angela was just a few steps past the door when Tuttle caught up with her. I couldn't hear what they said, but he ended up carrying the plants to her car for her. Then they stood by the car and talked for a while. Tuttle's was all about customer service.

I drove by Angela's school that night after I got off work. I didn't have her new address, but even if I had, driving by the school felt less like creepy stalker guy than driving by her new place. That, and I didn't know where she was living.

I could tell which classroom was hers by the goldenrod growing beneath the window.

28

I found Porter in the kitchen, coaxing a red simmer into greatness.

"Angela showed up at Tuttle's today," I said.

"What was that like?" Porter tasted the marinara sauce he'd been stirring with a wooden spoon. He smacked his lips in satisfaction. "They say garlic is the secret to life, but I think it's actually marjoram and crushed red pepper."

"Better than it could have been," I said. "She was picking up some tomatoes."

"The Brandywine tomatoes?" Porter asked. He dumped a heaping plate of sliced zucchini into the sauce. "The forbidden fruit of

Peregrine Perch?" He smiled as he stirred the pot. "Oh, my, Wendell. You never told me Angela was such a saucy girl."

"She was just getting tomatoes," I said.

Porter spun around to face me. "Not just tomatoes, Wendell. She wanted the Brandywines, the tomato of the rebellion. This is a strong independent woman who isn't afraid to challenge the system. I never knew that about Angela."

"You never met Angela," I reminded him.

He offered the wooden spoon with sauce and one zucchini slice in it to me.

"No thanks," I said. I went on with my story. "All she did was get a dozen tomato plants. Then she left."

"Did she say anything else?" Porter asked.

"I tried to hug her. She told me I'd be better off hugging a tree."

Porter looked straight up, like a baby bird laughing while it was waiting to be fed.

"Who among us has not sought the companionship of our bark-covered friends?" he asked. "Especially when we have an itch that we just can't reach. I could go for some hot back-scratching tree action right now."

"I don't think that's what she had in mind," I said. "She and Tuttle seemed to hit it off, though. I guess that makes sense. They both like plants and hate the Algos. I'll have to ask her about that when I see her again."

"Wait!" Porter spun around on one heel. "What about this other woman? What about Erica? Oh my." He tasted some of the sauce from the wooden spoon and continued stirring.

"The plot, like my sauce, thickens."

"There is no plot," I told him. "Erica is a friend. Angela picked up tomato plants. That's as thick as it's going to get."

I was desperate to change the subject, so I went to the only place I could think of.

"How's the table coming along?"

"Quiet nicely," he said. "Thank you. I've got the legs all together and all the same height."

"A very important thing for legs," I agreed.

"They're going to be about an inch shorter than they were, but you won't notice it. Now I've just got to figure out how to fix the tabletop without it looking like I just slapped a giant patch in the middle of it."

"We could always just get a tablecloth," I offered.

"But I would know it was there, Wendell. We might fool everyone else. Maybe Angela and her contraband tomatoes wouldn't notice. We might get past Pa or Lloyd, but I would know. I would know it wasn't right."

He shook his head and looked very sincere.

"I don't know if I could live with that," he said. "Don't know if I can live with that kind of deception. That kind of deceit."

"I see." I looked in the pot. "What are you cooking?"

"Speaking of saucy," he said. "I've got zucchini sticks toasting in the oven to go with these zucchini noodles I made last night. I think one of my clients might have found your stash. She greeted me with five more zucchini this morning."

"One marvels at your culinary creativity," I told him, "but I think I'm going to call Erica and see if she wants to get together for dinner. We need to talk about Leonard and all this zucchini stuff."

Porter waved a wooden spoon at me. "Met with the ex, now it's on to the next! Whoa!" He tapped the spoon on top of the saucepan of marinara sauce. "I had no idea you were such a player."

"Right. That's me," I said. "The Player of Peregrine Perch." I headed for the door. "I'm going to go over to Erica's."

I had just gotten to my car and was about to leave for Erica's when an official-looking black SUV pulled into the driveway and blocked me in.

Leonard got out of the back seat.

"Thought I might find you here," he said. "We've had a hard time finding your new address."

"It's temporary," I told him.

Leonard got right to the point, which, as usual for Leonard, was assigning blame.

"We've been backed up since you left us in a lurch like you did," he said. "None of this would have happened if I'd had enough people to check on things before they reached that point. And by 'enough people,' I mean you."

He paused, as if to give me time to appreciate what I'm sure Leonard thought was praise.

"I want to give you a job," he said.

"I don't understand you," I told him. "First, you tell me I have all these violations. Now you're offering me a job. Which is it, Leonard? Do you want to fine me or hire me?"

"You come work for me, and the violations disappear."

I felt my eyes narrow.

"So, this is one of those a 'nice life, Wendell. Be a shame if something happened to it' kind of things? Is that what we're playing here?"

"Something like that, yeah," he admitted. "I know it's not very original. It's a classic because it works. I'll give you a new title, say, 'Algorithmic Vegetation Coordinator' or something. And a raise. I'll even have the Algos design a nice little community garden where you can grow your vegetables and whatever."

"Thanks," I said. "It's so good to be appreciated."

"My offer won't last forever," Leonard warned. "I would encourage you to consider it." He smiled. "But I understand why you might want to talk to your girlfriend first. In fact, you probably *should* talk to her before you make any rash decisions. Since her career depends on this, I mean."

"My girlfriend?" I asked. For a moment, I thought he was talking about Angela. Then I remembered this was Leonard.

"You mean Erica?"

"See?" Leonard said. "It's that kind of perceptive insight that makes you such a valuable part of our Compliance team."

29

Erica was expecting me so I rushed over as soon as Leonard left.

"He must have gone straight from me to you," she said when I told her what happened. "He was here about an hour ago."

"Does this guy not have a phone?" I asked. "Email? A homing pigeon he uses as a courier?"

Erica sat on her front porch and looked up at me.

"He said that with you gone, they were going to be making some changes. They're moving me to Animal Waste Compliance."

"Animal Waste?" I echoed. Animal Waste was where careers were sent to die.

"Yes," she said. "In addition to poop cams in the park, I'll be monitoring kitty litter disposal boxes to make sure no one dumps clumping litter in the bins marked 'biodegradable only.' Apparently clumping litter doesn't biodegrade. Who knew?"

I sat down beside her.

"Oh!" She grabbed my knee. "And I get to monitor hamster cage disposal bins to make sure they're only using hypoallergenic recycled paper pulp in their cages and not cedar chips, because cedar disrupts the 'collective atmospheric harmony' at disposal sites, along with pine shavings, sawdust, even mulch."

She showed me an expression I had not seen her make before.

"All of this because you had your epiphany at Yellowstone," she said.

I tried to stop myself but I just couldn't.

"It was Yosemite," I said. "El Capitan is at Yosemite."

"I don't care if it was the Devil's Bidet," she said. "You had the epiphany and I get stuck with the litter box."

"The Devil's what?" I had to ask.

"I know," she said. "That's what my dad used to call this geyser in Yellowstone when we'd go up there in the summers. But that's not the point, Wendell. The point is, you quit and I'm the one who gets punished."

"He's only doing this to get to me," I said.

"I'll try to find comfort in that as I'm sifting through fake cedar chips." She smiled to let me know she was teasing. I was not convinced.

"So I should go back so you get your old job back?" I asked. "You said you hated that job."

"Hating a job and quitting is one thing," she said. "That's what you did. I hated my job and then I got moved to one even worse." She looked at me.

"I wanted to do what you did," she said. "To quit on my own terms. When it worked for me. That is very different than being reassigned to a department designed to get people to quit so the City won't have to pay their unemployment."

"I'm sorry," I said. "I don't know what to do."

As I drove away, I noticed more cars than usual in the Farrier Parking lot. The park had no soccer or softball fields that would attract that many people at the same time. It was just a place for people to exercise and just hang out. It wasn't designed for community events.

I stopped to see what was happening.

The Regulars were spread out all along the zucchini-lined pathway. Some were standing. Others sat in folding chairs, on top of ice chests, or just on the ground. Some were knitting. Others were reading. Others were just talking to their friends and neighbors.

Mr. Schneider was sitting between Ida and another woman and seemed to be enjoying the company of both, along with a few other Regulars who were laughing along at whatever he was saying. It was good to see the Leader of the Regulars holding court again.

Members of the tai chi class sat in the lotus position up and down the line. They were joined by families with children of all ages. Shaggy looking skateboarders. Nerdy-looking people who'd brought at least two books. Several dogs were also among their ranks.

Churchill was there and awake. Fred, however, was sleeping in his folding nylon chair.

"Nice to see you," Mr. Schneider said. "There's beer in the cooler."

They were all staring at a yellow backhoe parked near the zucchini. The backhoe looked newish, like it hadn't been used for anything worse than scooping mulch onto a playground. Like it had no idea of the atrocity it was about to be asked to commit.

The Regulars stopped talking when someone saw a man in a reflective yellow vest coming their way.

"Here's what's going to happen," Leonard said through the bullhorn as he approached. "You're going to move those chairs and all that other stuff you brought with you." He pointed to a dump truck parked by the maintenance shed.

"In a few minutes, a dump truck will arrive." Then he pointed to the backhoe. "Then this backhoe is going to take mulch out of that dump truck—more pointing—and bury every bit of the unauthorized vegetation that is on this pathway."

"Including the kale?" someone shouted.

"Including the kale," Leonard said into the bullhorn.

"Because the kale was already here," said the anonymous older voice. "I believe it was approved by the Algos."

There were general murmurings from the crowd about the approval of the kale, complete with historical references.

"Yeah," said another over the crowd noise. "The city planted that years ago."

"The kale's done nothing wrong," said another voice, this one an older woman. "You really shouldn't hurt it."

"The kale too!" Leonard said. He turned to the maintenance shed and waved the bullhorn like a flag.

He turned to the gardener's shed.

"Bring the truck!"

It was beautifully choreographed. The dump truck, a bright white truck emblazoned with the Peregrine Perch city logo, proceeded slowly across the yard. Jason, the park gardener and involuntary driver of the truck, pulled up slowly and stopped on the opposite side of the park, far away from the Regulars and their protected zucchini. There was a grinding of gears, then the dump truck crossed the track to the park's main lawn.

Jason could have driven straight across the lawn to where Leonard was standing. Instead, he chose the same arc that Banjo used when he was herding the puppies. The dump truck swung out wide, almost touching the kale border on the north side of the lawn. It came around in another slow arc, straightened it up, and headed up the middle of the field like a slow motion football player.

Leonard waved his arms like the guy at the airport who tells planes where to park.

Jason drove right past him. The dump truck kept heading south until it reached the track at the end of the lawn. Then it arced back to the east and traveled at less than a walking pace to the center of that side of the track. The truck turned to face Leonard and the Regulars head on.

Jason began his final approach. He stopped the truck about a foot from Leonard's feet and climbed out of the cab.

"I thought you said we were going to dig all this up," Jason said.

"No," Leonard said. "I told you the plan was to bury it."

Jason shook his head. "Well, that's not good." He walked over to the scoop on the front of the backhoe.

"I didn't bring the burying bucket. I brought the digging bucket."

"What's the difference?" Leonard demanded. "Just flip over the dirt and bury this stuff."

"The difference is that this one digs and the other one scoops," he explained. "You can't scoop with a digger. I'll have to take this back to the city shop and change buckets."

Leonard threw the bullhorn to the ground.

"And how long will that take?" he demanded.

"Couple of hours, if everything goes right and I have all the bolts. It's been a while since we used that bucket." Jason looked at his watch. "I'll be back here around nine-thirty."

"Can't you just use this bucket?" Leonard demanded. "We're burying zucchini, not building a highway."

Jason shook his head. "I cannot. Algorithm Compliance Code, Section 778, paragraph M, I believe, forbids the use of city vehicles for any purpose other than their intended and designated use. This scoop is intended for digging. You need a scoop designated for burying."

Leonard fumed.

Jason was unmoved.

"I'm sorry," he said. "I would hate to be out of code compliance."

Leonard put his bullhorn about a foot from Jason's face.

"I am the Code!" Leonard screamed into the bullhorn.

Jason was unfazed. "I'd have to consult the city attorney about that." He put his hand on the bullhorn bell and lowered it until he could see Leonard's face. "But for now, this Municipal Employee Union member is going to take this backhoe back to the city shop and get the correct bucket for this job."

I could see Jason's smile from where I was sitting.

"Sorry, Leonard, but that's what's going to happen," Jason said.

Leonard raised the bull horn like he was going to say something else but then just put it down and walked away.

Ida made sure everyone got some zucchini before they left.

I caught up with Mr. Schneider.

"Got a minute?" I asked.

He stopped walking.

"I owe you an apology," I said before he turned around. "I'm the reason you have multiple code violations. I was the one who wrote you up for the milkweed."

He looked confused. "You what? Why would you do that?"

"I used to work in Compliance," I told him. "I was the Landscape Compliance Officer. If you still have those notifications, you'll see my signature at the bottom."

His mouth drew a tight line across his face. He didn't say anything for a moment. His eyes narrowed.

"You're the reason we don't have Monarchs on the Perch?"

"I am," I confessed. "The Algos set the Algorithm. I verified and signed notifications before they were sent out. That was my job before I started walking dogs and working at Tuttle's."

"So, you were just doing your job?" he said. "That's your excuse?"

It didn't sound like much of a defense when he put it like that. It sounded like I was complicit in the crime.

"I'm sorry," I said.

"Yeah." Mr. Schneider smirked. "Me too," he said. "Sorry about all those caterpillars that people squished beneath their feet before they could become butterflies." He looked at me and shook his head. "You understand that Monarchs only eat milkweed, right? Not a lot of alternative dietary choices for Monarchs out there."

"I did not know that at the time," I told him.

"You just knew that the Algorithm said no more milkweed?" he asked. "Did they bother to tell you why? Would it have made a difference?"

"No, sir," I said, unconsciously reverting to my upbringing. "The Algos never explained anything to us. Maybe to Leonard or someone higher up, but not to the Supervisors. All they told us was that they were banned."

"My granddaughter loves butterflies," he said. "Now, if she wants to see them, I have to take her to the Butterfly Pavillion. You managed to cage even the butterflies."

He picked up his chair to leave.

"Mr. Schneider," I said. "I am very, very sorry."

"You should be."

30

I woke up around 4AM to the clatter of lumber hitting Porter's hardwood floor, transforming an otherwise pleasant dream into the nightmarish feeling of falling while you're still asleep. I felt the adrenaline surge as I jumped up in my bed.

"Sorry," he said as I entered the living room. "I needed to bring this in here." Porter, fueled by pride, patience, and caffeine, had been up all night working on the table.

He said he'd realized he wouldn't be able to carry the finished table into the house by himself around midnight. I'd only been home for about an hour and he didn't want to wake me. He decided to carry it into the house in pieces.

"And I appreciate that," I told him. It'd been a long day.

He'd figured out how to repair the table so the repair didn't look like a patch but was part of the design, in keeping with the wabi-sabi aesthetic he'd either embraced or just read about online. Then he rolled the round table top like a giant cheese wheel all the way across the yard from the work shed to the house and into the kitchen to assemble it there.

He carefully leaned the now slightly shorter table legs against the wall, but they ended up clattering their way to the floor.

That was what woke me: physics and the low coefficient of friction of Porter's hardwood floor.

I walked back out to the shed with him. He'd salvaged the original chair seats, thick pieces of wood with pre-formed butt-shaped contours. He'd replaced the shattered legs with dowel rods. Instead of rebuilding the chair backs, he'd opted for stools with no backs. It was a very practical, very *Porter* way to solve the problem.

"The first one took me about three hours," he said. "Measuring, adjusting the height, all that. The second one took me about thirty minutes."

He looked at the unpainted dowel legs.

"I'll paint these. Or stain them. Probably stain." He bounced up and down on one of the stools. "But that's for later. I have a dog to walk in two hours."

We carried the stools inside. Porter poured coffee for both of us from the pot he'd been drinking from all night. We sat at our kitchen table like civilized people for the first time since the deer incident. Even Banjo seemed more content.

"And how was your evening?" he asked as if getting up at 4AM was a normal thing.

I told him about the Great Zucchini Standoff, about Jason the Gardener's extremely aggressive passive-aggression with the backhoe bucket, and how so many people who used the park for so many reasons came together to take a stand for what I suspect was about more than just zucchini.

I left out the part about Erica.

"Nice." Porter took a long sip from his mug. "I take it you haven't seen this." Porter pulled out his phone and showed me a clip of Leonard screaming "I am the Code!" into his bullhorn.

It was beautiful. In less than six hours since it happened, Leonard's "I am the Code!" clip had 160,000 views; 43,800 likes; and 20,200 shares.

The parodies had already begun.

"This is all over the place," Porter said. "It's been looped, auto-tuned, captioned, you name it. I saw one where it rains zucchini and Leonard just keeps screaming until he's completely buried."

I laughed.

"Hashtag, I am the Code!" I said, as I sat on one of Porter's stools.

"Don't get overconfident," he warned me. "This is the part in the movie where the hero thinks he's won," Porter said. "He goes home. Feels good. Smiles in the mirror. Cue the music."

"I always like that part of the movie," I said.

He looked at me and lowered his coffee mug.

"But what the hero doesn't know," he said, "is that the villain isn't dead. He's just gone back to his desk. And now he's embarrassed."

Full stop.

"Now," Porter said, "if you'll excuse me, I'm going to try to get at least an hour of sleep before I have to walk Charlene Blacker's three beagles at seven. They're in crates in the work shed for the night."

I hadn't realized Porter was boarding dogs, but it made sense. He certainly had the room.

"They're spending a couple of nights," he told Banjo, "so you'd better behave."

"Want me to wake you up?" I asked.

"No. That's why I drank the coffee. I'll wake up when the caffeine kicks in."

Banjo was waiting by the door, jumping up and down in a tight circle like a bucking bronco. He would have opened it if he could have reached the door knob. I wasn't sure if he was excited about walking with me or if he couldn't wait to get to the beagles.

I drove by Erica's house and wondered if she'd be walking Biscuit that morning.

Apparently not.

The Regulars were already sitting guard along the zucchini vine when I got there. Banjo and I skipped the track and walked straight across the lawn toward them. The grass still showed tire tracks from the dump truck and the backhoe.

From the looks of it, some of the Regulars must have stayed all night. Several had blankets. Ida was pouring coffee from one of those red coolers with the little white spout, the kind you see at soccer games or construction sites.

I wanted to apologize to Mr. Schneider again, but he was not there.

A tuba player—technically a sousaphone player with a very nice brass instrument—was walking around with his instrument on his shoulder.

"Just in case Leonard shows up again," the tuba player told me. "But I can't decide whether to play Jaws, the Darth Vader theme, or the Skipper's theme from Gilligan's Island."

"Perhaps a tasteful medley of all three," I suggested.

The tuba player seemed to like the idea. He was still working on smooth musical transitions between the songs as I walked away.

Ida was inspecting the zucchini.

"Any sign of Leonard?" I asked.

"No," she said. "But it's early. Give him time." She kept inspecting the zucchini and didn't look up.

A city truck rolled slowly along the track. It stopped when it reached the zucchini. A young woman stepped out, clipboard in hand, wearing the official compliance office uniform: red polo shirt with black jeans. Her vest read *INTERN* in stenciled letters that looked like she had to change markers while she was writing it.

The Regulars watched her approach like a flock of pigeons evaluating a child with bread. The tuba player played Jaws.

"Good morning!" she said brightly. "I'm here to conduct a site evaluation."

"Of what?" Ida asked.

"Of the green space," the intern said. She glanced down at her clipboard. "And the unpermitted plant matter currently present in the kale corridor."

"The kale corridor," Ida repeated. "You make it sound like an airport terminal with a salad bar."

"I'm just here to take notes," she said. She walked the distance of the zucchini vine, but she seemed more interested in the people along the path than she was in any produce. Then she got back in her truck and left.

"She's the goat in the minefield." Ida said as we watched her drive away. "Leonard sent her in first to see if anything was going to blow up." She turned to me.

"It's not cruelty if it's procedure, right?" she said. I wondered if she'd been talking with Mr. Schneider.

I checked the oak as soon as I got to work. More brown leaves. More leaves on the ground. No matter how much I nursed the root ball, the patient was going to die unless we got it a permanent home soon.

"Have you seen this?" Tuttle held up his phone just as Leonard was screaming "I am the Code!".

With 1.3 million views.

"It was more impressive live," I told Tuttle. "Have you seen the one that's auto-tuned?"

"I talked to Jason this morning," Tuttle said. "He said Leonard threw a fit when he couldn't get the right bucket for his backhoe."

I pointed to Tuttle's phone. "That's the fit part, on the video. But I wasn't sure if Jason couldn't use that bucket or wouldn't."

Tuttle laughed. "A bucket's a bucket," he said. He looked at the tree and frowned.

"Leonard isn't going to let this go," Tuttle said. "You know that, right?"

"Porter said the same thing," I told him.

"Porter's smart." Tuttle walked toward the greenhouse. I went back to work trying to make the oak as comfortable as possible.

Around eleven, a black SUV pulled into the parking lot. It didn't look like the kind of car that you would use to carry anything with a little dirt on it. Too shiny, too official-looking. A woman in a business suit got out, carrying a leather portfolio like she was headed to a board meeting rather than a plant nursery.

She walked straight to me.

"Wendell Jones?"

"That's me."

"You've been served." She handed me the envelope, turned around, and walked back to her car without another word.

Tuttle appeared at my elbow, still wiping dirt from his hands.

"What's that?"

"Looks like a big birthday card," I said. "Shall I open it and see?" Despite my best efforts, my hands were shaking a little as I opened the official City of Peregrine Perch envelope.

"It's a compliance violation," I told Tuttle. I looked at the document. "From the City of Peregrine Perch, Department of Algorithmic Compliance. Complete with Leonard's signature and everything."

Tuttle stood beside me and read along as I continued.

"Here's the important part." I pointed to the line on the page so Tuttle could read it for himself.

"Total fine: $2,847.00."

"That's almost a full month's pay," I said, as if Tuttle didn't know what he was paying me.

"Seems a bit excessive," Tuttle said. "But did you expect anything less? Leonard is one of those guys who mistakes procedure for purpose and power for righteousness. He's focused on systems, not people."

Tuttle and I reviewed the itemized list of my compliance violations. Instead of one fine for the flower trail, Leonard had charged each flower in the trail as a separate offense. At that rate, it had taken only three flowers for me to make the bonus round of "repeat offenders" and the exorbitant additional penalties that came along with that. That was before he added fourteen zucchini plants, each as their own offense, all considered repeat offenses. There was a fine for "attacking the dog waste disposal container" from my first walk with Biscuit.

I wondered if Mr. Schneider had received a similar list. Or Erica.

"I'll give him unauthorized planting," I said. "That was kind of the whole point of this. But conspiracy to defraud? How do you defraud someone with a zucchini?"

I looked at the notice again.

"I can't pay this," I said. "Even if I could, I wouldn't. This is crazy."

"He's using you to prove a point," Tuttle said. "And he's probably enjoying this on some weird Leonard level."

I did my best to not think about my pending legal troubles and the potential risk for Erica and Mr. Schneider while I unloaded sod from a flatbed truck. The stacked rolls formed a wall that I wished I could hide behind and disappear.

I looked over my sod fortress wall just in time to see the same official-looking black SUV that visited Porter's the night before pull into Tuttle's parking lot.

"Well, look at that," Tuttle said. "It's the Code."

Leonard's eyes shot daggers at the older man but he ignored the comment.

"Did you get your notification?" Leonard asked. "I'd hoped my assistant would find you here."

I came out from behind my wall.

"What do you want, Leonard?"

"I already told you." He smiled. "I want to give you a job. I trust you've talked to Erica?"

"Which is it, Leonard?" I asked him. "Do you want me back or do you want me to pay these fines? Those are mutually exclusive propositions." I took the folded notification from my pocket, wadded it up, and threw it at Leonard's feet.

"I'll be sure and send you another copy of that for your records," Leonard said. "You're going to want to remember this for a while."

"Thanks," I said. "Wait. I have something for you, too." I pulled out my phone and showed him one of the "I am the Code!" clips.

"You're a star," I said.

Leonard lunged for my phone but I dodged his reach. He closed his eyes and took a deep breath.

"I'll hold off digging up the zucchini for a few days while you decide," he said, as if he was doing me a favor.

"How many days?" I asked.

Leonard laughed. "I'm not going to tell you that, Wendell. You'll know when it happens."

Leonard walked to his car. The driver had the engine started before he'd opened the door.

"Like I told you before," he said before he got in the car, "you're not the only one whose future depends on this."

"And if I come back," I asked, "will you cancel these fines for Erica and Mr. Schneider?"

Leonard, who was already crouching to get into the car, froze.

"What makes you think I sent notices to Erica or this—who was it? A Mr. Schneider?—or to anyone else?" he asked.

"I just assumed you had," I said. "Was I wrong?"

"You were," Leonard said. "But that sounds like a really good idea. I'll get right on that." He got in the car and rolled down the window.

"Same deal," he said. "You come back, their violations disappear. It's all up to you, Wendell."

Tuttle and I stood in silence as Leonard's car drove away.

"Has Leonard always been so… I don't know.. so *Leonard?*" I asked. "Normal people are not born that way."

Then again, normal people don't set up their friends for outrageous punishments like I just had.

Tuttle didn't answer right away. He uprooted the weed and tossed it in the wheelbarrow with the other weeds he'd pulled from the gravel parking lot.

"I've known Leonard Bixely a long time. When they first hired him, they put him in charge of a community garden downtown. A little square space for tomatoes, another for eggplant, some green beans and cucumbers. It was nice." Tuttle brushed his hands together and smiled.

"And they bought all the plants and seeds from me," Tuttle said.

This was the first I'd heard of this.

"What happened?" I asked.

"Leonard discovered that rules mean power," Tuttle said. "Once that happened, he was more interested in power than he was in plants or people."

Tuttle put the wheelbarrow down.

"He stopped seeing people," Tuttle explained. "In the beginning, he'd bring his lunch to that community garden. Or he'd help himself to a tomato or a cucumber right off the vine and have that for lunch. People would come by to pick up a zucchini or with questions and Leonard would help them."

"Then the Algos started adding more regulations," Tuttle continued. "Leonard went from telling people how to properly stake their tomatoes to telling them which varieties they could and could not plant. He stopped coming to the garden after that. Said he didn't want to deal with people anymore."

I did the math.

"That must have been when he was promoted to Compliance Supervisor," I said.

"I don't know about all that," Tuttle said. "I just know that he stopped having lunch in the garden and then he stopped coming by here for seed and plants. After that, he only came by if he suspected I was selling plants that were out of compliance."

He looked and pointed at me.

"And then you started coming around with all this Algorithm stuff."

"The Algorithms came with Leonard," I tried to explain. "He made this big presentation about how Algorithmic Compliance would make for a better customer experience."

Tuttle's eyes narrowed. He smiled slightly as he turned to me.

The older man shook his head. "Was that the term he used? 'Better Customer Experience?' They're not customers. Customers are easy to persuade or even to ignore. These are homeowners. They have invested in the community. They deserve to decide which plants they want in their yards."

I picked up the wadded up notification and wondered what the Leonard I never knew would have said about that. I also wondered what Angela would think if she knew about my current life of crime and my $2,847 in fines and potential criminal charges. She'd probably make some crack about me overcompensating again.

She'd love the goat rodeo that was yet to come. This was my first violation, but I'd testified at several landscape violation hearings on things ranging from the acceptable height of junipers (not to appear overgrown or to block windows in any way) to what color chrysanthemums may be paired with different colors of houses.

Residents could paint their house whatever color they wanted, as long as they wanted brown, slate blue, or taupe.

My rodeo would involve a lot more goats than either of those cases.

The notice said I had ten business days to respond, which basically meant ten days to admit I was guilty and pay my fine. Failure to pay a municipal fine like that could, potentially, mean they could take my driver's license or garnish my wages, neither of which really fit into my schedule at that time.

I could simply send in a check. For all its Algorithmic brilliance, the City of Peregrine Perch still hadn't figured out how to take payments online. Or so they said. Those of us who worked in Compliance knew this was a feature, not a bug. The inconvenience was part of the punishment. Late fees were a revenue stream.

Or, if I preferred, I could challenge the ticket and have my day in court, or, more precisely, have my day in an administrative session. I still had to contact them within ten days and notify them of my intent.

I still wasn't sure what I intended.

31

I got home in time to see Banjo herding three beagles around the fenced-in part of Porter's back yard. At least Banjo was herding. The beagles looked like they were playing tag.

Porter watched the dogs while he cooked.

"For the record," he said as he stirred the saucepan, "zucchini does not work as well as butternut squash for ravioli."

"Thanks," I said. "I'll be sure and warn the others."

Banjo cornered the beagles in a back corner of the dog yard.

"Excuse me," Porter told me. He stepped out into the yard.

"That'll do," Porter said in a calm voice. Banjo immediately stood down while Porter rescued the puppies. He patted Banjo on the head and gave him a treat. He put the beagles back in their kennels.

I tried not to think about Leonard and the notification, but I couldn't get what he'd said out of my mind. I could save myself and Erica a lot of trouble if I went back to work. Erica seemed like a good person. I could help her out. But I wasn't sure I wanted to work for the Code just so she could keep her job. I felt guilty for even thinking that, but that's how tired I was of working for this guy.

Porter filled up a plate with zucchini ravioli and went outside to eat. Before he sat down, he released the beagles again.

"Get 'em," he said.

We ate zucchini spaghetti and watched.

Banjo put his head down and moved low and fast toward the pups. The beagles, still thinking this was a game, ran in three directions. Banjo didn't chase. He ran the same arc pattern that he did with the deer and corralled the puppies back to the kennels. One even went inside.

"That'll do," Porter called out. "Good dog." Banjo clocked out from work and walked over to where we were sitting.

"Good dog," Porter told him. He dropped a few spaghetti noodles on the ground for Banjo to eat.

"That's amazing," I told him. I leaned against the doorframe. Banjo was ready to go again.

"I've been working with him as much as I can," Porter said. "Saying 'that'll do' instead of 'heel.' We're still working on 'come around.'"

He looked at me and moved his fork as if he was tapping on some unseen nail in the air.

"It'd be great if you'd start doing that when you walk him," he said. "Just say, 'that'll do' when you want him to stop. Don't yell it. Just say it nice and calm."

"That'll do," I practiced.

Banjo cocked his head and looked confused.

"And 'get 'em?'" I asked. "Where did he learn that?"

"He already knew that," Porter said. "My guess is that those kids who owned him before thought it'd be funny."

"He's doing great," I said.

"Yeah," Porter said, "but the beagles go back tomorrow. He's going to need something else if I'm going to keep training him."

Banjo and the beagles entertained us until dark. Then we kenneled the beagles. Banjo pranced in front of the kennels on his way to the door; one last reminder of who was boss.

"Come on, Banjo," Porter said. "Let's go to the shed."

I was scrolling on my phone because we still didn't have a TV. It wasn't that we'd made a conscious decision to step away from cable. More like we had both realized we didn't need it, especially now that there were so many Leonard videos to watch. I settled back with one of Porter's zucchini donuts. They were exceptionally good, with some kind of glaze that I was sure only Porter could create.

I decided to go to the shed to thank him before I went to bed.

Porter was contorting himself to reach beneath whatever he was building, like he was adjusting a drawer. It was too tall for a coffee table and not tall enough for a workbench. It was something in between, which was why Porter was having such a hard time reaching the drawer. His chair wasn't tall enough for the job and the table wasn't tall enough for him to stand. Four fresh cut pieces of wood stood propped up on the workbench next to him. A crumpled tarp was on the floor.

"What's this?" I asked.

Porter didn't even look up. "Just a little project," he said as he kept measuring.

"This is quite the workshop," I told him. "Do you ever sell any of the things you build?"

He stood up. "Used to, before I got busy with dog walking and all this other stuff. Buyers have expectations. Delivery times. Now, I just build things I want to build when I want to build them."

"And you don't sell them?" I asked.

"Somehow," he said, "it feels like they're worth more when I don't."

I touched the unsanded wood.

"And this is something you wanted to build?"

"It is." He just smiled, went back to work, and offered no other explanation.

I took my violation notification to the *Elbert County Tribune* the next morning. The *Tribune* had the entire violation on their website by lunch, under the headline:

BECAUSE OF SOME ZUCCHINI???

The story included a photo of Mr. Schneider smiling and holding up a zucchini in a pose usually reserved for fishing tournaments.

They also included a link to the "I am the Code" clip, now with 3 Million views and 85,000 shares.

I got a call from the Mayor's office the next day, from an assistant who barely waited for me to say hello before she launched into a cheerful-but-firm explanation about the importance of uniformity, oversight, and the "evolving relationship between citizens and data."

Her entire introduction had all the markings of an AI response.

"I'm calling because I hear there's a problem in the park," she said.

I told her about my single coneflower and how it was removed. I told her about how Mr. Schneider and I built the trail, about the scroll, and about the manzanita tree.

"And that's when you decided to go with zucchini?" she asked.

"It seemed like the next logical step," I said.

"I will pass all this along to the mayor," the assistant told me. "Is there anything else you'd like for us to know?"

"I don't suppose you can help me with these fines that Leonard is hitting me with," I asked.

"The mayor does not get involved in individual cases. I'm sure you understand," she said. "You should contact municipal court and schedule a time for your hearing."

"I will." And, in fact, I did—as soon as I got off the phone. They scheduled my administrative hearing in just two weeks.

"You may, of course, change your mind at any time and simply pay the penalty," the scheduler said. "If you do that, we'll drop the court date. And of course, until that time, this will appear on your credit report as potential financial liability."

"Of course it would," I said. I was still trying to wrap my head around "simply paying" three thousand dollars for planting a few purple flowers and some zucchini.

32

Porter was a polite insomniac, even after he saw me sleep through a tornado siren and had to wake me to go to the basement. There was no way he was going to wake me by doing anything in the house. But even though he knew that, he was still very careful about making any sound when I was sleeping.

"Nobody respects sleep more than people who do not sleep," he said.

By the time I made it to the kitchen that morning, Porter was already in the backyard hosing down dog crates while Banjo played in the water.

"Expecting guests?" I asked.

"Something like that," he told me. "They picked up the beagles this morning, so I thought I'd clean these up and try something."

"This morning?" I asked. "How early do these people get up?"

"Not as early as I do," Porter said.

I got Banjo's leash and headed to Farrier. I wanted to see Erica. I was hoping Erica wanted to see me.

Banjo and I had just entered the park when Mr. Schneider, Ida, and some of the other Regulars saw us and waved us over to where they were gathered. They were looking at a shiny new and very official-looking bulletin board with a bright red metal frame, complete with a locking glass case for notices.

"There's Mr. Johnson," Ida said. She gasped and put her hand over her mouth.

"And Mrs. Rivas!" Ida said. "Look!"

"Algorithmic Violation: Non-standard native grasses," Mr. Schneider read. "Second offense. $175."

It was a list of Algorithmic Violations up to last week. I knew that's what it was because it said "ALGORITHM COMPLIANCE VIOLATIONS – PUBLIC NOTICE" on the frame above the glass.

The violations were listed by date and went back a couple of months, starting with Mr. Johnson and the rosebush incident.

Mr. Schneider pointed to my name and gave a low whistle. He looked at me as if there was another Wendell Jones that might have received that kind of fine.

"That's me," I said. "I need to stop being such an overachiever."

He laughed softly and patted me on the back.

"I'd say we're even," he said.

I looked at him for a moment. Then we both went back to looking at the list.

The violations weren't just for landscaping. Erica's Algorithmic Language Compliance Violation for her social media comments was also listed.

"They hit you for $100 for that?" I asked. She hadn't told me how much the fine was.

"Yeah," she said. "That cost me."

Noticeably absent, at least to me, were fines for Erica or Mr. Schneider's participation in my crimes. Leonard either forgot or he was holding those cards back for later.

"Must have slipped my mind," said another one of the Regulars. "I don't remember getting a violation for that," said another. There were 256 violations in all.

"I already paid my fine," Ida said. "There's no reason for them to post it like this."

"It's intimidation," Mr. Schneider said. "The Algos want people to know that there will be consequences for misbehaving."

A notice at the bottom of the sign read, "Compliance keeps Peregrine Perch beautiful" and a website where people could report violations.

A woman that I thought I recognized walked over and hugged Ida. She was about my age. From the way she was dressed, I assumed she was a lawyer.

"Did you know anything about this?" Ida asked her.

"I did not," she said. "This must be coming from Leonard. My office had nothing to do with this."

Ida must have felt me eavesdropping. She turned around and called me over.

"Wendell Davis," she said, "this is Monica Crespin, my daughter."

"How do I know you?" I asked as I reached for a handshake.

"She's the mayor," Ida said. Ida beamed with motherly pride.

"Nice to meet you," said Mayor Crespin.

"Nice to meet you," I said. I pointed to my name on the bulletin board.

"I'm your highest earner," I told her.

Mayor Crespin smiled and asked if I knew Leonard.

"I used to work for him," I said. "Then I quit."

"And that's when these fines started?" she asked.

"Well, yeah," I said. "But, to be fair, that was also when I started planting flowers and then the zucchini."

"The zucchini Leonard wanted to dig up?" the Mayor asked. She looked at the list of fines again. "This does seem like a disproportionate response," she said. "These were flowers, not felonies. At least they shouldn't be felonies."

She hugged Ida.

"I've got to go, Mom," she said. "But thanks for telling me about this."

I went home to get ready for work. I looked through the sliding glass door and saw dog crates in the back yard.

I opened the gate and let Banjo outside before I saw the chickens.

Six chickens.

Loose.

In the yard.

Banjo froze, one paw up like a pointer, ears locked in, tail straight as rebar.

"No," I said. But that was the wrong command.

The chickens looked up in slow, synchronized horror.

Then chaos.

Feathers launched like popcorn in a microwave bag. One bird tried to fly. Another hid under a folding lawn chair. A third somehow made it on top of one of the dog crates.

"Let's see what he does," Porter said.

Banjo dropped to a crouch, his tail doing helicopter circles like he was trying to generate lift. Once he'd decided on his strategy, he started in a brisk walk. He tried to form a perimeter around the screaming flock, but the chickens refused to organize themselves into anything like a circle. Unlike sheep, who seem to instinctively know how to circle the wagons for protection, this was every chicken for themselves. The loud, high-pitched squawking sounded almost as if they were screaming "Run!" at the top of their little chicken lungs.

Porter stepped a little closer to the action.

"That'll do," he said.

Banjo looked confused and disappointed, but he stopped his patrol and trotted to Porter's side. The chickens settled down and returned to the food that Porter had poured out for them earlier. Porter ushered Banjo into the house and closed the door behind him.

"You let the dog out?" he asked.

"I didn't know we had poultry," I told him.

He shook his head. "You didn't read the text I sent you?"

"You sent me a haiku about eggs," I said. "I didn't know what you were talking about."

"That *was* the text," Porter said. "I thought that was very clear." He recited his haiku:

Six hens on the run,

scrambled before any eggs.

Dog still wants the jam.

"No one appreciates ancient literary artforms anymore," Porter said. "Give me that blanket in that chair over there."

The chickens scattered as Porter approached. He didn't run or try to chase them. Instead, he waited until he was close to one of them and tossed the blanket over the bird.

"Come on, Eggatha Christie," he said to one of the chickens. "Now you, Miss Beakley."

"Did you suddenly have a craving for eggs?" I asked. "You don't even eat eggs."

"These are not for us," he said. "These are for Banjo." He put the struggling Mr. Beakley into his crate. "If he can herd chickens, he can herd anything."

Porter found another chicken and an egg hiding under a chair next to the door.

"Thank you, Miss Marple," he said.

"What are you going to do with the eggs?" I asked. The chickens calmed down enough that even I could pick one up and put it in the cage before Porter answered my question.

"I thought a lot about that while I was setting this up," he said. "We don't have a rooster, so these eggs won't be fertilized. There's no risk of cracking an egg and having a naked chick fall into your omelet."

We both sat on the repurposed dog crates.

"So you're going to start having eggs for breakfast?" I asked.

"Me?" He laughed. "No. But you can. And that lady with the sourdough starter might like some. And Pa. Maybe I'll sell them at the Farmers' Market on Saturdays. Maybe I'll just give them away."

I knew a little about chickens from one we had in our classroom when I was in second grade.

"They lay an egg every day," I reminded him.

"Not always," he said, "but, yeah. They're prolific. We're going to need some egg cartons."

"And you're okay with using these for Banjo's entertainment?" I asked. "Doesn't that seem just a bit cruel?"

"I prefer the term *collaborative learning experience*," Porter said. "We're going to have to go slow at first." He looked at the egg he'd collected from Miss Marple. "If they stop laying eggs, we'll know we're stressing them out. But Banjo is a natural. He just needs somewhere to develop his chops."

I looked at the time and drove as fast as I could to Tuttle's so I wouldn't be late.

33

After work, I called Erica and asked if she could meet me at Farrier Park.

"You realize I'm still mad at you, right?" she said.

"I know," I said. "I'm just hoping that you're not as mad at me as you are at Leonard."

"That's a pretty low bar," she said.

"I like realistic goals," I said.

Most of the Regulars had gone home by the time I got there. A few remained, sitting in lawn chairs, simultaneously guarding and distributing zucchini. One sign advertised free zucchini bread. Ida offered a piece to me.

"No thanks," I told her. "Porter's made plenty."

A grandmother waved a posterboard sign proclaiming "#I AM THE CODE!" as I walked by. We laughed together.

Erica and Biscuit walked across the lawn to join us.

"Everything okay?"

"Yeah," I said. "I just wanted to say that none of this would have happened without you."

"That's not true," she argued.

"Yes, it is. I was walking Biscuit when I saw that first coneflower. I was walking Biscuit when I planted the first flower for the trail. So, no matter what happens, thank you for that."

"I talked to that vet today," she said. "I told him I wanted to leave Compliance. He asked when I could start." She smiled. "I gave Leonard my two-week notice."

"That's great!" I told her. "What did our dear former leader say?"

"He said, 'Don't bother with two weeks.' So I called the vet. I start tomorrow." She smiled and wiped a tear from the corner of one eye and smiled.

"For the first time in a long time," she said, "I'm not dreading Monday."

"Even better," I said. "Congratulations!" I knew I still had work to do, but this seemed like a good place to start.

Mr. Schneider and his granddaughter were sitting a few feet from Ida. I wanted to tell her that she'd also been the inspiration for a lot of this, but I also didn't want to tell her that her grandfather had shared her homework with me. Still, it was nice to have a face to go with the scroll.

"You just missed Leonard," Mr. Schneider said. "And he was looking for you."

"Me?" Erica asked.

"No," Mr. Schneider told her. He turned to me. "He was looking for Wendell. Sorry."

I nodded like that was fine. It wasn't. Leonard didn't show up in public unless he wanted to make a point—like burying the zucchini or offering me my old job back. He liked to do his work from the home court advantage of his office. On away games, he was zero for two. He would not want another loss.

I was about to leave when I heard the roar of a diesel engine, followed by the grinding of gears and a low, mechanical growl from the park work shed.

Leonard was driving a snowplow.

In June.

He stopped just short of the first zucchini and stepped out of the cab. He was wearing a hard hat and an orange vest with the words "Algorithmic Landscape Enforcement Division" stenciled on white tape across the back.

"Step back!" Leonard said into his bullhorn.

"This is an active landscaping correction. Please step back."

No one stepped back, so the Compliance Supervisor stepped forward.

"This is your final warning," he said in the infamous bullhorn. "You are interfering with an officer and the performance of his duty."

The only sound was the engine on the snowplow.

He walked back to the snowplow.

"Wendell," he yelled before he climbed in. "Anything you want to say?"

I looked at Mr. Schneider. He silently mouthed the word, "No." I looked at Ida. She did the same.

"I regret that I have only a few hundred zucchini to give for my country," I said.

The blade scraped the ground like a knife across dry toast, peeling up kale, slicing through zucchini, and removing half the compost in one pass. The blade's V-shape design pushed this earthy mixture in two directions, digging up ground and burying half the pathway in the process. Exposed roots writhed like tiny worms on a concrete track.

Biscuit whined softly. Erica didn't speak. Mr. Schneider just stared straight ahead.

Leonard spun the snowplow around and pushed what was left of the dirt and vegetation into a pile by the chess table. Then he drove across the lawn and out to the parking lot.

The Regulars reacted like medics in a war zone, collecting the injured, determining what could be saved and what could not, deciding what could be baked into bread and what would be left to become mulch and squirrel food. An older man held half of a large zucchini while he searched for the other half. A young girl kneeled alongside a bright orange zucchini flower and cried. Another grimly collected the fallen and gently put them in a basket.

Ida stood up. "What was that?"

I looked at Mr. Schneider.

"That was Leonard telling me not to bother coming back," I said.

34

The Regulars slowly realized there was no way to repair what Leonard had destroyed. Ida folded her blanket. Mr. Schneider wrestled with a canvas chair that wouldn't go back in its bag. The skateboarders picked up trash but—with no approved bags on hand—left it in a pile beside the can.

I looked at the destruction and wondered what I had done.

Mr. Schneider gave up on the chair and reached out to shake my hand.

"We had a good run. Thanks, Wendell."

"For what?" I asked. "For building everyone up so they could get plowed? For making Erica have to find a new job? I'm not sure what you're thanking me for."

"Don't be so hard on yourself," he said. "This meant something."

I didn't argue. I just said goodbye and headed for the parking lot. Erica followed me, but neither of us said anything. My hands were still shaking as I opened the door to my car.

"You okay?" she asked.

"No," I said. "I'm glad you got that job. I'm just really tired. I think I'll just go home and try to get some sleep. Maybe this will all look different when I wake up."

Porter, the world's least predictable Algorithm, was sitting on the couch watching something on his phone when I got home. He'd rebuilt the couch frame but hadn't solved the cushion problem. A bench was better than nothing.

"Hey there, Mr. Ecoterrorist!"

"You think this is funny?"

"I think it's hilarious, but I'm a little warped." He slapped the bare bench of the couch. "Sit down." He showed me his phone and the video he'd been watching.

"Tonight, ecoterrorists defeated at Farrier Park," said Sally James, Denver's most Algorithmically optimized news anchor.

"Zucchini as a weapon of ecoterrorism," I said. "Is TSA going to start asking if that's a zucchini in my pants?"

The video—shaky and zoomed—showed Leonard plowing up the garden. Someone from the newsroom must've called him. They'd dubbed his voice over the clip.

"We've been watching this particular ecoterrorist cell for some time now," Leonard said over pictures of the Regulars shuffling away from the snow blade. "Monitoring their activities. Trying to reach a peaceful resolution to their demands. But in the end, we had no choice but to take action against what was clearly an ongoing threat."

"Thank you, Leonard Bixely," Sally James said. She turned to Camera 3.

"And now in sports..."

"It's over," I told Porter. "You heard her."

"What?" Porter laughed. "The only people who think this is over are the ones who get their news from Sally James."

"You get your news from Sally James," I reminded him. "Everyone in the state gets their news from Sally James."

"Some people watch because they believe it," Porter said. "The rest of us watch because we can't believe it's on TV. Trust me. When normal people see that video of Leonard using a snowplow to take out some zucchini and some old people, they're going to go crazy."

"This is my fault," I said. "All of it. If I'd just taken his offer…"

"Stop being such a narcissist," Porter said.

"But the timing." I told him about Leonard's offer and about Erica quitting.

"The timing is Leonard being Leonard," Porter said. "He probably decided to fire Erica before he asked you to come back. What you were going to do never mattered. He just wanted to see how far he could push you. It's entertainment to him."

"At least nobody got hurt," I said.

"Everybody was already hurt," Porter said. "They just didn't know it. They'd been hurting so long they didn't recognize it anymore." He leaned forward. "You think Mr. Johnson was happy when they took away his rosebush? You think Mr. Schneider was happy when they humiliated his granddaughter? Do you think any of this was working?"

I didn't say anything. I didn't want to remind him I was the one who sent Mr. Johnson his violation notice. I was the ominous "they."

Porter went on. "You had two weeks where people were truly happy with something they were doing. Two weeks where nobody worried about lava rock or weed height or their roses being labeled noncompliant."

I looked at him. "And we got a lot of zucchini."

"We got a lot of zucchini," Porter echoed. "The most versatile of the squashes."

Porter was right about one thing: By morning, the video of Leonard snowplowing the zucchini was on track to become even more viral than his "I am the Code" video. There were split screen versions, mashups of the snowplow video with Leonard saying "I am the Code," and remixes. The original "I am the Code!" clip was being attached to the end of all kinds of videos as a kind of ironic joke.

A new video variant emerged the next morning.

"My granddaughter wrote a beautiful letter," Mr. Schneider said on a reel that came up while I scrolled. "They called it a violation. I am not the Code."

I swiped left and saw Ida and two other Regulars.

"We shared zucchini with our neighbors. We are not the Code."

I swiped left again. It was Angela.

"I protected a student who wrote about losing his hamster. I am not the Code."

That one made me pause. There were 28 more in that thread alone.

Porter stuck his head in my bedroom.

"What are you stirring in your coffee today?" I asked.

"Some of that leftover tahini," Porter said. "It's like almond milk, but more committed." He sat down on my bed, barely missing my shins.

"Have you seen these?" I asked him. "They're going to wish the Guerilla Gardener was all they had to contend with."

A mother with a baby on her hip told her camera, "I planted lettuce because I couldn't afford to keep buying it. I didn't know there was a rule. I am not the Code."

There was. And a $50 fine, if I remembered correctly. I was probably the one who verified her violation.

I scrolled a few more reels until I saw one that made me stop and watch it again.

"I am the Code," said an angry man in a baseball cap. "If people followed the Code, none of this would've happened. We wouldn't have a big rut where the kale used to be and the track wouldn't be covered in dirt."

I looked at Porter.

"He's right, you know."

"Sure," Porter said. "Everything's easier when you color inside the lines. But it isn't really art, is it?"

Porter closed my door as he left. I got ready for work.

"Peregrine Perch has a problem," announced John Musgrave, the morning voice of Peregrine Perch radio. "Looks like we've got a caller. Phil? You're on the air."

"Hi, John. Long time listener, first time caller." It was an older voice. I wondered if Phil was one of the Regulars.

"The problem is the Algorithms," Phil said. "A friend of mine was fined $500 for a rose bush. Another had to remove a beautiful willow tree because it was five inches from the sidewalk. They told him it could be no closer than six."

"And you blame this on Commissioner Bixely?" Musgrave asked. Leonard wasn't technically a commissioner of anything, but facts were never a problem for John Musgrave or his station.

"I do," the caller said. "He's fining people for everything. There shouldn't be any fines at all, not for stuff like this. It's ridiculous. It's…"

"Thank you for your call," Musgrave interrupted, silencing the voice of dissent. "You want amnesty for these criminals? Have you never heard of broken window theory? Small problems, when ignored, lead to bigger problems. If you don't nip it in the bud" —he paused to laugh at his own joke—"you'll have people rioting in the streets."

The talk show host was just winding up. "If Leonard Bixely is guilty of anything, it's of not putting a stop to these weapons of ecoterrorism sooner."

Musgrave took another caller.

"I agree with the previous caller," the caller said.

"So you support amnesty too?" Musgrave laughed. "What is this? Anarchist morning?"

"We should drown Leonard Bixely in daisies, or whatever noncompliant flower you might choose," the woman said. "Make it so there are so many violations that Leonard can't possibly keep up."

"You could do that," Musgrave said. "Or you could move to another community where there is no law."

I turned off the radio. I could figure out traffic on my own.

I made it to Tuttle's and checked on the oak. Despite my best efforts, the tree was looking more lethargic every day. Tuttle was talking about selling firewood in September. If it was going to have time to cure, it would have to be cut long before then. I wasn't sure I had the arms or the heart to cut up a tree like that by myself.

Later, when I was watering the parsley, a woman asked about creeping thyme.

I felt my eyes dilate.

"Where do you live?" I asked.

"Why does that matter?" she asked. Her face said that she knew exactly why it mattered.

In a world where zucchini is a bioterrorist weapon, creeping thyme is a slowly unfolding nuclear device. The plant has no respect for boundaries. As the name implies, it creeps in non-conforming, non-Algorithmic spread patterns. It's like a camel with water and can thrive without sprinkler systems or even much rain for weeks.

But the Algos stated that lawns were to be covered in Kentucky Bluegrass, even though we lived in a semi-arid climate that was running out of water. Creeping thyme, a native plant that thrived in Colorado's thirsty climate, was labeled as an "Uncontained Propagation Risk" and banished from the kingdom.

I knew that because I helped write the regulation.

"Using this for groundcover?" I asked.

"Yes," she said. "I intend to cover as much ground as possible."

I smiled and said nothing.

"So, if you don't mind, I'd like two hundred and forty plugs of creeping thyme," she insisted. "Can you give me that or not?"

"I can." I walked with her back into the nursery. She bought all one hundred eighty of the creeping thyme plugs we had.

"I can have more for you by tomorrow," I told her. As the day went on, we sold every plug of blanket flower, a beautiful but unpredictably self-seeding plant that wreaked havoc on the Algos' perfectly manicured lawns. We sold poppies, bachelor buttons, and cosmos—all banned because they were hard to contain and control. All were suddenly very popular.

"This is crazy," Tuttle said. "Any idea what brought this on?"

"You got some free advertising from John Musgrave," I told him. "One of his callers, anyway."

Ida arrived at Tuttle's on a bus from the Senior Citizen Center. She and her fellow travelers bought an assortment of plugs to plant, including several plugs of black-eyed Susan. When we ran out of flowers, I started selling vegetables. One woman bought a seventy-two cell tray of lettuce. We sold completely out of every variety of peppers.

By three o'clock, Tuttle was calling his suppliers with emergency orders. By the time we closed at six, the only thing left in the greenhouse were some houseplants. Even the "top secret" Brandywine tomatoes were gone.

Tuttle sold more restricted plants that day than he had since I started working there.

But he froze like a Marine called to attention when someone asked for honeysuckle.

"Don't sell it," Tuttle said.

"Why not?" the lady asked. "You're selling sunflowers and I know they're banned."

I stopped to listen.

"Sunflowers are banned for aesthetic reasons." Tuttle, the man who loved plants, suddenly sounded like a seasoned Compliance Officer. "No other reason than the Algos decided they didn't like how they looked. They're native to Colorado and provide a lot of food for birds and squirrels. I'd sell sunflowers all day if they'd let me, along with all the other banned plants I sell."

"So why not honeysuckle?" she asked.

"It's an incredibly invasive species," Tuttle tried to explain. "Emphasis on 'invasive.' It'll choke out the plants that were meant to be here."

The woman became indignant. "I thought you hated the Algos."

"I do," he said. "But I try not to take it out on the other plants."

I enforced Code because it was my job. Tuttle was enforcing something much older—stewardship of nature.

As we finished the day, I wondered if the flowers I'd sold might end up in Farrier Park. Maybe they were already there. I decided to drive by there on my way home.

I didn't make it to the park.

The lawns across the street from Farrier were an explosion of color—poppies, blanket flowers, creeping thyme—bursting from neat little plugs like confetti, all two to six inches apart. A mix of random colors, textures, and shapes that broke every Algorithmic Landscaping Code on the books and probably a few that were yet to be written.

The sheer volume of it was overwhelming. Even if I hadn't quit, it would take a crew of compliance officers a week just to write the citations. With no compliance supervisor, that might stretch out to August.

I could only imagine how Leonard would react.

35

The nursery was usually closed on Sundays so Tuttle could have a day off. But he'd never had a Saturday like that before. Tuttle asked if I'd help unload all the plants and flowers that came in to replace everything we sold in the Saturday rush.

Porter was straightening a tarp that covered something in the back of his truck when I went outside to leave.

"Is this what you were building?"

"It is." He stopped. "I don't usually do this, but would you like to have a look? I'm kind of proud of this one."

Porter removed the tarp. "It's a flower box for Jill. Or a vegetable box, I guess." He ran his fingers across the polished wood.

"It's whatever kind of box she wants it to be."

He climbed into the truck bed and sat on the side.

"If I sit like this, it's about the same height her wheelchair would be." He reached across the box. "She can reach right in there, dig around, play in the dirt. And if she can't reach something, she can always wheel herself around to the other side and get to it from there."

"That is amazing," I said, because it was.

"Yeah." He looked very proud of his creation. "I built three. I figure Jill's not the only frustrated gardener over there."

It was a nice start to my day. Then I left for work.

The Sunday Morning radio crew was only slightly less obnoxious than their weekday counterparts.

"What's going on over at Farrier Park?" Roger Dodger asked, followed immediately by audio of Leonard saying "I am the Code!"

"Doesn't look that way to me!" said The Dodger. "Now, traffic on the nines."

Tuttle looked happy but still in shock when I got there.

"Now I know how grocery stores feel when there's a blizzard warning," Tuttle said while we waited for the truck. He smiled. "What a beautiful mess."

Most of the nursery floor was dirt to begin with, so it was impossible to say what had been relocated and what had always been there. Loose soil clung to the edges of shelves and piled up in corners, coating the lower shelves and any surface not meant to hold soil. The tiled areas inside the building and around the front counter were covered in mulch and mud, with ruts from shopping carts and smeared muddy footprints.

The shelves that held vegetables and outdoor flowers were empty, save for a few wilted stragglers whose rejection seemed too painful to bear. Houseplants stood unmoved in the shaded parts of the store, like guests at a party who never made it into the room where the cool kids were.

Saturday had been all about outdoor planting. We'd sold a few pots of rosemary, dill, and some other herbs, but nobody was thinking about repotting anything. Every single clay pot was still there, along with enough terracotta saucers to serve an army.

The outside tables looked picked over, like the last day of a large yard sale. Most of the tables were empty. A few sunburned marigolds and one broken tomato cage stood as proof that something had once happened here. All that remained were stacked bags of potting soil.

The truck driver opened the door, and we got to work.

"Your friend across town had the same kind of crowd, but he doesn't carry anything that isn't code compliant," the driver said while he helped us unload. He smiled at Tuttle.

"Sucks to be him."

We were about halfway through the truck when I realized what I hadn't carried inside.

"No sense in ordering vegetables," Tuttle said. "Too late in the summer for that. And it's too early for pumpkins and things like that. I wish we'd had more in stock. We could have sold it all."

Since I was there anyway, I checked on the oak. There were more dead leaves. A twig snapped off in my fingers.

Erica called to ask about lunch. I told her I was helping Tuttle. She showed up about thirty minutes later with a sandwich. I pulled up some buckets, and we sat by the oak to eat.

"Chris told me something you might find interesting," she said.

"Chris? You mean Chris Schneider?" For some reason I always thought of him as 'Mr. Schneider.' I don't think I've ever called him Chris. Just seems wrong, somehow.

"Okay." Erica swallowed the last of her sandwich. "That's weird. You're a grown up now. You can use people's first names. But that's not what I was going to tell you."

"Sorry to interrupt. Continue."

"He said that one of the Regulars started a page to get donations for your legal fees."

I didn't know what to say. I'm sure my jaw dropped. I probably closed my eyes and shook my head.

"They didn't have to do that."

"He said you'd say that." Erica put her hand on mine. "They want to do that. You should let them."

"I'll have to thank him."

"It's not just him," Erica said. "Ida was there and some of the others. You should probably thank all of them."

"And you didn't put them up to this?"

"I think they took a look at a guy who quit walking dogs so he could work at a nursery and figured he probably didn't have an extra three grand laying around to pay a violation fine."

Tuttle was looking at us, so I told Erica I should get back to work.

"I see how you're looking at her," Tuttle said later. "If you're going to do it, you need to do it now."

I assumed he meant Erica. "I know. It's just…Angela.. all that…no…"

"What?" Tuttle said. "The tree, Wendell. I'm talking about the tree."

Tuttle walked a slow, lopsided circle around the crown of the oak, inspecting it like it was a gently used car with the potential to be more. Checked a leaf. Tried to bend a branch to see if it would break. He made his way back to the root ball and me.

"You've been thinking about this since you started working here," he said. "Like some kid with a crush on his homeroom teacher. I didn't say anything because I really wanted to sell this tree, but that's not going to happen. And I'm not selling it to that contractor guy for $300. We might as well put it to good use."

He waited for me to say something. That was optimistic thinking on his part. I had nothing to say.

"Do I need to spell this out for you?" he asked. "I will give you the oak. You can plant it in Farrier Park." He sighed like this was costing him money, which it was. At least three hundred dollars. Two thousand dollars, if by some miracle we might manage to sell it that afternoon.

"I'll even help," he offered.

"That would certainly be something bigger," I said. I hadn't expected him to give up the tree.

"You're going to need my hydraulic spade. I'll operate that. You can drive the flatbed with the tree on it over there. It'll take at least five of us to do this. We'll need your friends to help."

"I just happen to have five friends, counting you."

"I'm not your friend," Tuttle said. "I just think you're okay. He rubbed his temples. "You help me load it, we get it over there, then we plant it. That's the deal."

"Should I call them now?"

"We don't need them right away, but make sure they're ready for tonight. You and I should be able to get this on the flatbed. The hard part comes later. That's when we'll need your friends."

I called Porter and Erica. "The guerilla goes big time!" Porter said when I asked him. I'd have to ask Mr. Schneider when I walked that evening.

"We're going to need someone to cut the lights," I told Tuttle, as if he hadn't already thought of that. "I don't know anyone who can do that."

"Jason will take care of the lights," Tuttle said. "I'll talk to him."

Tuttle brought out some rope and some straps to tie everything down.

"Let's get as much of this done now so we don't have to rush through this tonight," he said. It was clear that by "we," he meant me.

I disconnected the drip line. I spent that afternoon wrapping more burlap around the root ball to keep it from drying out and to keep it safe. I tied the smaller upper branches together to keep them from breaking off. I removed enough of the brown leaves so we wouldn't leave an obvious trail along the way.

Tuttle inspected my ropes and redid a couple of my knots.

"Now hitch the trailer to the truck and bring it over here."

The truck was older than me. It was held together with defiance and rust. The motor started just fine, but the transmission cried out in pain when I tried to put it into first gear. I managed to drive the twenty or so feet from behind the nursery to the tree lot without killing the motor or running over anything.

Tuttle did not look impressed.

"Please tell me you know how to drive a stick."

"I'll tell you whatever you need to hear," I said.

After a few missed attempts, I managed to back the truck up to the trailer and get everything hitched.

"And this is why you and I are not friends," he said. "Can you drive it or not?"

"I can drive it," I assured him. "I just had a little trouble getting it into gear." *But don't expect a fast getaway if the police show up,* I thought.

The truck with the hydraulic spade was even louder than the truck I'd be driving. The spade looked like a giant claw on one of those grab-a-toy machines. I was glad Tuttle was running it because I've never had good luck at those things.

The spade claw grasped the root ball and gently laid it on the trailer with the roots touching the cab of the truck. I crawled underneath the canopy, much like Jack the Rabbit and other furry creatures that I'd been chasing away for the past two weeks, and guided the top of the tree while Tuttle pivoted the root ball with the spade. It was like he was turning a hand on a very large clock.

Once everything was on the trailer, I tied it down with rope and bright orange ratchet straps.

"Those orange straps kind of give it away, huh?" Tuttle said, as if a truck carrying a fifteen foot tree would be hard to miss.

"If they stop us, I'll just tell them we're moving it to Porter's place."

Jason recommended we do the planting at midnight. Something about less traffic around the park, but I think that was because he liked saying "Let's do it at midnight" more than for any practical reason. The park closed at ten.

Tuttle told me to go no faster than 35mph. Our little convoy left the nursery at ten-thirty. I led the way with the truck and the oak. Tuttle followed with the hydraulic spade. Apparently Tuttle didn't think I'd notice if a one ton tree suddenly fell off the truck. Porter rode in the cab with me.

Porter hung his head out the window and watched as we grazed the first traffic light hard enough to make it dance like a pinata but not knock it down. The stop sign on the next corner was not as fortunate. Neither was the shopping cart that was beside it.

"Was that in the budget?" Porter asked.

"Should've been," I said.

"You've got two more right turns and a left," Porter reminded me. "Try not to kill anyone."

It took us forty minutes to make the eighteen mile trip. I pulled into Farrier Park at eleven-forty. We parked behind Jason's service building at the north edge of the park. Porter had brought headlamps. Erica met us with energy drinks and a white shirt she'd tied to a stick to use as a flag.

"We could have used you on the way over here," I told her.

The sky was cloudless with a bright moon. The Perch was close enough to Denver that the city created a dome of light on the western horizon but far enough away that you could still see the Milky Way and several constellations if you looked away from the city. Farrier Park was about a thousand feet higher elevation than Denver. When you couldn't see the stars, you could always look at the lights below.

Jason cut the lights precisely at midnight. He then emerged from the gardener's shed and walked dramatically across the lawn. He checked a couple of my knots before he opened the cab door.

"I'll take it from here," he told me. "I don't want you running over anything."

The nighttime quiet was shattered when Jason started the truck. It only got worse when he put it in reverse. The truck beeped all the way from the service building to the middle of the lawn. Porter winced and pulled his black ski hat over his ears. Erica guided him in with a flag she'd made from a white tee shirt.

The giant hydraulic spade was much quieter by comparison, but only because Tuttle didn't have to back it up. He pulled to the middle of the lawn and started digging.

Erica got out her phone and started recording.

I unwrapped the root ball while Tuttle dug. The burlap that had retained the tree's water since it became homeless smelled horrible, but it was easy to get off. The wire basket that actually held the roots in place was another story. Porter used the same fencing pliers he'd used to fix Banjo's fence to cut through the wire mesh once the tree was planted.

Despite the noise of the spade's diesel engine, I still felt like I needed to whisper.

"He's either digging a hole for the tree or he's digging our grave."

"Or both," Porter practically yelled. "Tuttle is efficient like that."

Porch lights started coming on. Dogs were barking.

A police cruiser pulled up and parked on the street.

"There goes the neighborhood," Porter said.

Jason climbed out of the truck and walked toward the officers. He waved when they shined their flashlights on him.

The officers kept walking. Jason intercepted them before they reached the tree. I tried to hear what they were saying, but none of us could hear anything over the sound of the spade.

Then they went back to their car.

I met Jason before he was halfway back to the tree.

"What did you tell them?"

"That we were planting a tree. It seemed a little obvious."

"And they just walked away?"

"Said it sounded like a Leonard problem to them."

Every porch light on the street was on. People started walking over.

Ida and Mr. Schneider were the first to arrive. Then some of their friends, more of the Regulars. They wore bathrobes and sweats, slippers and orthopedic sneakers. A police car shined a flashlight as it drove by and caught me square in the face.

He did not stop.

It took Tuttle about twenty minutes to dig a hole five feet deep and three feet wide—big enough for a fifteen foot tree to call home.

"Looks good," Tuttle said as he walked around the hole. Jason drove the flatbed until the root ball was next to the oak's new home.

Tuttle lifted the ball with the spade while Porter and I guided it into the hole. Erica and Mr. Schneider provided a Greek chorus of warnings. At one point, the tree tipped and caught me in the shoulder. Not hard, but enough to remind me that it was alive and heavy and not quite convinced this was a good idea.

Finally, when everything was right, Tuttle dropped the tree in its forever home.

He adjusted the spade a few times to make sure the tree was as straight as possible while Jason passed out shovels. I removed the wire and the burlap that was above ground, checked the branches, then stood back and let myself look at it.

Jason pointed to the gardener's shed.

"There's about 150 feet of water hose curled up over there," he told Erica. "Go get it and bring it over here. And try not to get too wet."

Porter tied four padded guy lines around the trunk, took fifteen paces for each, and drove the stakes into the ground while Tuttle and Erica pulled on the lines on opposite sides of the tree. Jason moved his arm to give some idea of the up and down alignment. Porter nailed down the stakes once it was as straight as we thought it was going to get.

We mixed mulch with the dirt and filled in the hole. Then we scattered a few stray twigs and leaves around the trunk to make it look like it had always been there. I unleashed the hose and made sure the ground was soaked.

The oak looked magnificent in the moonlight, a fifteen foot silhouette backlit by the dramatic glow of Denver's lights. Tuttle looked like a proud father.

"I told you it was a beautiful tree."

There were no celebratory speeches. No poems by Walt Whitman or anything like that. Just handshakes, pats on the back, and tired nods. I heard Jason whispering, "That was cool," like some kid who'd just set off illegal fireworks in a mailbox.

Porter and I took the truck with its empty trailer back to the nursery. We counted only two downed stop signs along the way.

The tree was in the ground, whether Leonard liked it or not. Tomorrow, people would see it and be happy.

And for the first time in a long time, that was enough.

36

The tree was the second biggest thing to happen to me that night. When we got home, I witnessed—for the first time—Michael Porter, insomniac extraordinaire, say goodnight and disappear into his bedroom to sleep.

He didn't even stop to pet Banjo. Just yelled, "Good night, Banjo!" and went to bed, leaving me to deal with the dog's separation issues as he paced behind the glass door.

I was almost through the kitchen when Porter stepped back into the living room.

"We did good tonight," he said. "And you! You didn't just capture the flag. You planted it in the Horde's front yard and told them to water it."

Then he yawned and disappeared. Just like that.

I went outside. Banjo wasn't the only one who needed to calm down.

"I think I just declared war on Leonard." I rubbed Banjo's head. "Think he'll show up and ransack our house?"

Banjo barked.

I reminded myself that the dog heard inflection, not words.

In hindsight, I don't know how I missed it. I guess I'd been so wrapped up in saving this dying tree, so worried that I would kill the one responsibility I had left, that I hadn't given much thought to how Leonard would react. After losing Angela, losing the house, and essentially losing my job because of Leonard, I was just focused on not failing again.

I needed to keep that tree alive just to prove that I could.

I needed a win. And this was a very big win.

"But did I really have to plant a tree in Farrier Park?" I asked Banjo.

What I meant was, "Given my current legal problems, can I really afford to upset Leonard more than I already have?"

If he was fining me almost three thousand dollars before, then what would he do now? I thought about all the violations I'd committed by planting the tree—violations that *we'd* committed, because I wasn't the only one I'd put at risk—and wondered what the final tab might be. The Regulars may decide to use their fundraiser to pay their own legal bills once Leonard started passing out notifications. Erica might never speak to me again.

At least Angela would know I was no longer Mr. Compliance. Then again, so would Ben. So would our mother. I was not ready for that conversation. It was easier to think about how Leonard was going to come after me with everything he had. At least that was predictable.

He might not even wait until morning. Leonard might not know how to operate a backhoe, but he could drive a snowplow. Ordinarily, I wouldn't think that a snowplow could take on an oak tree, but this was a freshly planted tree. Sitting in mud.

He'd probably cut the guy wires and push it over himself. Leonard would love that. Pretending he's the Hulk or something. And then he'd love telling the story over and over again, probably even more than he loved to tell us how he climbed El Capitan. Future compliance officers would use me as an example of the cost of noncompliance.

"Good!" I said to myself. "At least they'll know there was a time when people stood up to the Code. I started thinking about what I could plant if he killed the tree. I was fairly certain that another fifteen foot oak was not going to drop in my lap. If Leonard killed it, I would need to find something to replace it.

You really can't go back to coneflowers once you've planted a tree.

37

Banjo's devotion to routine notwithstanding, I wasn't going to go to Farrier Park the next morning. I wanted the tree to be alive for as long as possible, even if it was only in my mind.

I did wonder if Leonard would have it hauled away as soon as it fell or if he would let it lie there to bleach in the sun, like a skeleton on a battlefield. I wondered, but I wasn't curious enough to want to see it for myself.

My phone dinged. It was a text from Erica saying that I needed to get to the park "NOW!!!".

I set my phone face-down and reached for coffee.

Porter glanced up from his mug—dark roast, caramel-infused rice milk, a reckless sprinkle of cinnamon.

"You going?" he asked.

"So I can talk to Leonard?" I said. "No thanks."

Banjo tilted his head with a look that asked why we weren't on the way already.

I sighed and grabbed the leash. Porter refilled his mug and came along.

I turned on to Farrier Parkway. The street was lined with more flowers and plants than I had ever seen. I parked the car about a block from the park and Porter, Banjo, and I got out to walk. Yards along the street were decorated with assorted fresh plants and plugs from Saturday's mass flower revolt. Less than twenty-four hours earlier, these were all on shelves at Tuttle's. With so many, I wondered if other nurseries hadn't been hit, too.

Erica and Biscuit met us at the entry to the parking lot. I took a deep breath as the five of us crossed the parking lot and headed into the park, like our own little family.

The tree still stood.

Not only was the oak still standing, but people were gathering around it. Not a mob, not even a crowd, at least not at first. They were just people, some alone, some in little clusters: two women sharing a blanket while one read aloud; a dad sitting on the ground, rocking a stroller with one hand and holding a book with the other; teenagers in the shade sharing earbuds. Someone was sketching in a notebook, someone else was reading.

The Regulars sat in their lawn chairs and watched the sun rising behind the not-quite-yet-mighty oak. The slow motion dance of the tai chi group echoed the movement of the branches. Runners pivoted their heads as they passed.

Mr. Schneider sat on a blanket on the ground, his granddaughter curled beside him, sketchbook in her lap. He wasn't looking at the tree; he was watching people gaze at it. He raised his mug towards me, a kind of coffee drinkers wave, nodded, and smiled.

I smiled and nodded back.

Ida was making sure everyone had a loaf of zucchini bread. Jason checked the guy wires and packed more dirt around the base of the tree. There were no signs, no plaques. No yellow ribbons. Just a tree.

And Angela.

I hadn't seen her come into the park, but there she was, all smiles as she walked towards the tree from the other side of the lawn. She looked happy, like she'd seen a friend. For a moment, I thought she might have seen me. Then I assumed it was a student or a parent.

And then she walked up to Tuttle.

And then she hugged him.

I blinked. When I opened my eyes, they were still there, him with his arm draped over her shoulder; her looking leaning into his side. They stood there, together, looking at the tree like a very happy couple who were just getting to know one another.

I laughed. Porter was right. She was a saucy girl after all. Good for Angela.

Leonard stood proudly beside the scar where the zucchini had been, scanning the crowd like he was calculating how many citations it would take to clear the place and who should get theirs first.

He obviously had not seen me.

People drifted in. Dogs and dog walkers who had to investigate. Runners who wanted a closer look.

Leonard said something into his phone, waited for a response, then slowly walked back to his car.

Another car pulled up in a few minutes. It was the Mayor.

Her Honor and Leonard approached the tree. Leonard power walked five to ten steps ahead of Mayor Crespin. The Mayor walked at her own pace and did not appear to be in a hurry. You would have thought it was a Fourth of July parade the way she waved at the crowd as she walked up to the tree.

Leonard raised his bullhorn.

Before Leonard could speak, Mayor Crespin reached out—calmly, silently, and without so much as even looking at Leonard—and lowered the bullhorn. Then she took it from his hand. She handed it to the intern and whispered something to Leonard that I couldn't hear. Leonard immediately started walking back to the car. Ever the politician, Mayor Crespin smiled and worked the crowd while Leonard sulked in the backseat.

"What just happened?" I asked Ida.

"I'm not sure," she said. "But I have it on good authority that Leonard is going to take a mental health break while the City reviews the Algorithms and these fines."

She smiled.

"But you didn't hear that from me," she said.

Banjo circled the trunk once, declared it safe, and flopped into the shade. Porter laid down beside him and gazed up at the sun. Ida was chatting with Erica and Mr. Schneider was laughing with his granddaughter. Other people were talking, laughing, and sharing zucchini bread.

All because of a single purple coneflower that dared to show up where it wasn't supposed to be.

I wasn't ready to plant another flower. Not yet.

But I knew I would.

Other books by Bob Seay

Literary Fiction

The Bookseller's Son

When a small-town Arkansas bookstore becomes a battleground in a war over banned books, Jeremiah Malone is caught between defending his parents' legacy and choosing his own path. A story about community, courage, and the power of words.

Dad

When Jacob Martin gets a late-night call to retrieve his elderly father, what starts as a rescue turns into a cross-country odyssey of memories and unexpected connection. A funny, poignant story about caregiving, second chances, and the ties that keep us together even as time pulls us apart.

The Band Room

When high school football star Angel Rivera is sentenced to ninety hours of community service, the last place he expects to end up is the band room. As friendships deepen and long-buried truths surface—about his family, his school, and himself—Angel faces choices that will determine the kind of man he becomes. A heartfelt story about identity, second chances, and finding your place where you least expect it.

Cozy Mysteries

Drawn to Murder

Street portrait artist Gabriella Alegré loves the lively chaos of Boulder's Pearl Street—until a fellow busker, a world-class flutist playing for tips, is brutally attacked. His priceless platinum flute is missing, and suspicion falls on his closest friend. Drawn into the investigation through friendship, curiosity, and maybe a little stubbornness, Gabriella uncovers rivalries, obsessions, and long-buried secrets in Boulder's art and music scenes. A cozy mystery with humor, romance, and an artist's eye for detail, *Drawn to Murder* is a story about creativity, community, and the unexpected places the truth can hide.

Portrait of a Murder

They hired her to paint a family portrait. They didn't mention the killer might already be in the frame. When street artist Gabriella Alegré takes a lucrative commission from one of Boulder's most prominent families, what should be a career break turns into a murder scene. Smart, warm, and slyly funny, *Portrait of a Murder* blends cozy-mystery puzzle solving with an artist's eye for telling details and a sharp sense of community. Perfect for readers who like their whodunits with heart, humor, and a heroine who refuses to look away.